BTL C   S|19

This book should be returned/renewed by the
latest date shown above. Overdue items incur
charges which prevent self-service renewals.
Please contact the library.

Wandsworth Libraries
24 hour Renewal Hotline
01527 852385
www.wandsworth.gov.uk

Wandsworth

also by Beth from MHM Publishing

coming soon

Fleabag and the Fire Cat (book 2)

Fleabag and the Ring's End (book 3)

For younger readers

The Dragons of Kilve

and for older readers

THE STAR DANCER QUARTET

STAR DANCER
FIRE DREAMER
WAVE HUNTER
STONE KEEPER

Fleabag

& the Ring fire

Best wishes
Beth Webb.

written and illustrated by

Beth Webb

MHM
March Hamilton Media

www.marchhamilton.com

LONDON BOROUGH OF WANDSWORTH	
9030 00006 7219 7	
Askews & Holts	23-May-2019
JF	£6.99
	WW19000560

ISBN 978-0-9576626-1-2

MHM
March Hamilton Media

In memory of our wonderful mum
Peggy Webb – with love

and in tribute to the many cats who have wandered
through my life.

Thanks (as usual) to Andy, Chloë, Julie and Lucinda
for making this new edition possible.

1 Strange Fire

The tongues of flame reached higher and higher. There was no sound or smell of burning, but Gemma could feel heat against her cheek.

There were other people there too. She didn't know them, but their faces dimly reflected the orange and yellow glow.

'One day,' she told herself, 'I shall know what it all means.'

Gemma rubbed her eyes.

She often saw strange things when she looked into the depths of the queen's Ring, but the pictures were different every time. The opal's crimson fire seemed to be burning in another world far away – yet the huge stone was only just beyond the end of her nose.

Every morning, when Gemma brought the queen her tea, she watched the Ring's strange fire and tried to understand what she saw.

Today, the pictures seemed to be urging her to *do* something… but what?

'Don't look too long into the Ring Fire, little one.

You are too young.' The queen touched Gemma's shoulder and smiled.

Gemma jumped. 'I'm sorry your Majesty, I was daydreaming.' She curtseyed, poured the tea, then pulled back the curtains. Sunlight flooded the room, turning the old lady's silver hair to gold.

'Shall I fetch your clothes, ma'am? Today is the last day of the Great Festival. Perhaps you'll find your successor at last?'

Queen Sophia yawned. 'And perhaps I will not. To tell the truth, I'm sick of this festival. I've had wrestlers fighting to show how a monarch must beat all opponents, poets writing long and exceedingly boring elegies on the nature of royalty, runners bursting their lungs winning races to show that a sovereign must be… something else, I can't remember what.' She smiled wearily.

Gemma's eyes sparkled. 'I liked the knights who wanted to kill dragons or rescue princesses to show how brave and strong they are.'

'They did look rather fine with their armour all polished,' the queen agreed, 'but it's a long time since we had any marauding dragons. In fact we haven't had one since – oh, when I was quite a young thing. It was all terribly exciting.'

The queen sighed and sipped her tea. 'Anyway,

they're all missing the point. None of them has the remotest notion of what it really means to rule. Oh, they *talk* about strength and wisdom, but all they really care about is having lots of money and everyone obeying them.'

Gemma longed to ask what the point *was*, but she didn't dare.

The queen nodded towards her desk. 'Fetch today's programme and read it to me, please.'

'Yes ma'am.' Gemma picked up the embossed paper. 'Today we have jesters, more poets...'

Her Majesty groaned.

'Some politicians, a wise man and a historian...'

The old lady groaned even more loudly.

Gemma glanced up nervously. 'Are you all right, ma'am?'

The queen rolled her eyes. 'Oh yes, but they're all so *boring*! Read on.'

Gemma began again, 'They all wish most humbly to represent to your Royal Highness their insights into what it means to be monarch of this land. Oh, and in pencil at the bottom, it says "The Royal Fire Welder".'

'The Fire Wielder,' the queen corrected. Then she almost dropped her teacup and sat up straight, her eyes sparkling. 'Is *he* coming? *When*?'

'It doesn't say, ma'am. But he's last. What does he

do? Is he a fire juggler? Oh, I do hope so. I saw some at the Midwinter Festival. They ate roaring flames and threw burning torches up into the rafters. There were sparks everywhere. It was so beautiful, I almost cried.'

'No. No. Nothing like that,' the queen replied, pushing her feet from under the covers. 'The Fire Wielder is important – without him I am nothing. Help me get up girl, as quickly as you can.' She perched on the edge of the bed, flushed, excited, and looking twenty years younger.

Gemma gawped, then remembering her duty, she took a sapphire-blue gown from the wardrobe.

Queen Sophia shook her head. 'No, no, child,' she laughed. 'I'll need my golden robes of state. I shall wear my crown and my emeralds. Send for my hairdresser and my lady's maid, oh and tell that pompous Prime Minister to oversee the festival in my place. He'll thoroughly enjoy himself. I have more important things to attend to.'

The queen's wrinkled face broke into smiles. 'This is going to be such a special day – perhaps the greatest of my entire reign!'

2 Look at Yourself!

The Royal Hairdresser was not hard to find and once Gemma had delivered all the other messages, there was nothing left for her to do except creep slowly and miserably down the back stairs to the kitchens.

Gemma longed to stay and see this 'Royal Fire Wielder' who'd made the queen so excited, but that privilege would be for the daughters of lords and ladies.

Gemma didn't even know whose daughter she was. Five years before, the queen's carriage had almost run over a smelly guttersnipe. Her Majesty had ordered the urchin to be taken back to the palace. The child had been washed, given a name, clothes and a job. She'd even been taught to read and write.

But as Cook frequently reminded Gemma, she'd come from the gutter and that was where she belonged.

Cook was fat, greasy-skinned and mean-eyed. He reinforced his opinions with the back of a wooden spoon slammed on any table – or servant – within reach, especially on bad days.

And today was likely to be very bad indeed.

Cook hated festivals. They always meant extra work. This made him drink too much cooking sherry. Then he'd get a headache. Headaches meant that everything anyone did would be wrong. As this festival had already lasted three days, Cook's headache would be quite severe by now.

Gemma shivered as she made her way down the servants' stair. The warm glow from the fire she'd seen in the Ring had long gone. Anyway, it'd only been a dream.

Her steps became slower, for each one brought her closer to her nightmare. She stopped where the stairs twisted to the right, bringing her to the servant's hall and into full view of the kitchen door.

'If only I didn't have to go back down there,' she whispered, rubbing a bruise on her shoulder.

Then she sat down hard and buried her head in her hands. She couldn't face being shouted at today. She hated being beaten for nothing. Perhaps she'd be better off going back to where she'd come from, living off market scraps and sheltering in doorways?

Just because she was housed and fed didn't make this a better life. She only stayed because she loved the queen.

At that moment, a warm softness twisted around her legs. Absent-mindedly, she reached down and scratched the old black cat behind his ears.

'Hello, Fleabag, how are you? I saved you some bacon rind. When Cook goes out, I'll get it.'

The cat nuzzled his ugly face into her hand. 'Let's go now,' he said. 'I have a little corner that needs filling.' He started to hobble downstairs on his three legs, but Gemma didn't move.

The cat stopped on the bottom stair, and looked back. 'You're scared,' he purred.

'How do you know?'

'Dead easy,' growled the cat. 'You're sitting out here on the stairs instead of getting me my third breakfast. Don't worry, Cook is at market, Manda and Jane have gone to help and Harry and Tina are scrubbing out the scullery. It's quite safe.'

Gemma crept nervously into the kitchen. The great pine table was scoured and smelled wet and sweet. The rafters were hung with polished copper pans, ladles and moulds. Between them swung bunches of herbs and baskets of eggs.

Suddenly Fleabag yowled and sprang across the room, his razor claws unsheathed. The grey mouse hiding behind the flour bin knew no more.

Gemma turned her back. She knew it was most

impolite to watch while a cat ate his prey.

After a few moments, Fleabag gave a small burp and a polite cough. 'Oh dear, excuse me. Um. A little chewy, but a good flavour. I must confess I let them get at the flour bin now and then. It does add to the quality of the final meal... Ho, ho, get it? The final *meal*?'

Gemma did not wish to 'get' such an awful joke and ignored him. 'Are you still interested in that bacon rind?' she asked.

'Later, thank you,' he muttered between licks at his paws. He was always meticulously clean. 'That mouse has filled the little space I did have. Perhaps you'll give it to me for elevenses?' he enquired hopefully, his shaggy black head on one side.

'Maybe,' Gemma replied, scratching under his chin.

'You'd better,' Fleabag mumbled as he resumed the examination of his fur and whiskers. Then he stopped and looked up at her. 'To be honest, I'm more interested in *you* than bacon rind.'

'What do you mean?'

'Just look at yourself!'

Gemma went over to the big mirror where servants were supposed to check their appearance before going upstairs.

'What's wrong?' She tugged her fair hair into a

tighter ponytail. Leaning closer to the glass, she rubbed at the freckles on her nose. No dirt there. She twirled around. Her brown dress was a bit long and baggy, but it was clean and mended. She straightened her apron and turned back to see the cat sitting on the table.

'Oh, you wicked animal!' She scooped him up. 'Cook will cut your other back leg off if he catches you up there!'

'Huh, I'd like to see him try.' Fleabag struggled free and landed heavily on the hearthrug. 'Now, come and sit down. I need to talk to you seriously.'

Gemma knelt next to the huge open fire, and Fleabag curled up opposite her, the firelight catching his golden eyes. 'Now listen,' he began. 'You know where you came from?'

'The backstreets.'

'Quite. Do you know where you're going to?'

Gemma shrugged. 'I'd not really thought about it. I'll stay here all my life, I suppose. When Cook gets cross I wonder about running away, but I know that's silly. My reading and writing is quite good, and Manda's teaching me to make pastry, so I might be able to get a job somewhere else. But I don't want to leave the queen.'

'And what'll happen to you when she dies?'

A lump swelled in Gemma's throat. She got up and poked vigorously at the fire, making sparks dance into the cavernous chimney. She looked over her shoulder at Fleabag. 'Do you think she'll die soon?'

The cat spread his whiskers. 'Don't you? She's very old and this festival is wearing her out. Cook hates you because you're the queen's pet. As soon as she's gone, you'll be given all the worst jobs for ever.'

Gemma shuddered.

'So, what do you suggest?'

The cat rolled onto his back, his three legs sticking out at ridiculously odd angles. 'You could start by scratching my tummy. That always helps me think.'

Gemma rubbed her fingers through Fleabag's fur. Delicious purring rumbled his fire-warmed body.

After a few minutes he twisted round and sat up. 'That's enough, thank you. Now, tell me, what would you like to do, if you could do *anything*?'

Gemma didn't need to think. 'I'd like to stay here and be a maid to the queen, or her successor, but you don't think that's possible, do you?'

'No, I don't.' The cat shook his head vigorously and a few dozy fleas landed on the rug. 'But I have a few practical alternatives. First of all, and right now, you must run upstairs. I hear Cook opening the back gate.

'Secondly, you must go and stand by the rose

garden entrance. There's a visitor coming up the path, you must let him in and take him to the library. The butler's busy counting the silver teaspoons and he gets into a terrible strop if he's interrupted.'

Fleabag twitched his whiskers. 'And thirdly, you must wait and see what happens next.'

'Jane! Manda!' Cook bellowed. 'Hurry *up*!' His big boots clomped across the courtyard.

Jumping up, Gemma leaped through the door.

Hoping to help give Gemma a head start, Fleabag tugged something limp and grey from behind Cook's chair, then with one bound he landed in the exact centre of the kitchen table.

Between his paws lay a smelly rat with yellow teeth. It was very dead and very ugly.

In the same moment, cook's bulk wobbled through the kitchen doorway. Fleabag jumped down and rubbed himself around the man's legs, purring and mewing for all he was worth to show his master the rat, neatly laid to view.

Cook took the cat's tail in one hand, and the rat's in the other. With a powerful swing, both animals were tossed through the door and into a heap in the middle of the herb bed.

Fleabag, whose tail was very tough, simply returned the rat to its hiding place. It was the same one he always brought out to impress Cook – or to annoy the butler. It did the trick although it was getting a bit smelly these days.

Returning to the garden, Fleabag twitched his whiskers in the sunshine and purred as the front door opened to admit a very special visitor.

3 The Fire Wielder

The little man on the royal doorstep was completely round in every way. Round stomach, round head and big brown eyes.

With a sweeping gesture, he plucked off his flame-red fez and bowed. As he straightened, a toothy grin cracked his face into a million laughter lines.

'Oh, good,' he said. 'You're here.'

Gemma was so astonished, she just stood gawping, leaving the stranger standing on the doorstep.

At that moment, Fleabag sprang over the threshold and rubbed his back against Gemma's legs. 'Pull yourself together!' he ordered. 'The butler is coming!'

The cat hobbled along the corridor into the dark gloom of the hallway with as much dignity as his three legs could muster.

Gemma curtseyed and spluttered, 'W-welcome, Sir. Whom do you wish to see? What name shall I give?'

The little man cocked his head on one side and considered Gemma with a quizzical smile. Without speaking, he held out his hand. In his palm flickered a tiny golden flame.

Gemma gasped and looked at him wide-eyed. 'The Royal Fire Welder – I mean Wielder!' With burning cheeks, she curtseyed again to cover up her fluster, lost her balance and stumbled over the butler's bunion.

With one motion he grabbed Gemma's arm and shoved her behind the door. Then straightening his green velvet jacket, the butler swept a perfect bow to the guest. 'Do come in my Lord,' he droned. 'If you would be so good as to wait in the library, Her Majesty will be with you shortly.'

As the Fire Wielder stepped into the marble hallway, the butler closed the door and kicked Gemma spitefully in the shins at the same time.

'Get down below,' he hissed, 'and don't let me catch you up here again. *Ever!* Get it?'

Gemma nodded, cowering out of sight and waiting for the visitor to pass.

But the Fire Wielder did not move. Instead, he stood dark and still, staring at the butler with a look that would have withered an oak tree. 'I wish to be attended while I wait,' he said firmly.

The butler bowed again. 'Certainly sir. I shall be at your disposal.'

'By that young lady behind the door.'

The butler glanced over his shoulder at Gemma's

huddled form.

'I'm sorry, sir. You should not have been embarrassed by the sight of a mere scullery maid. She had no right to be above stairs. I will summon one of the ladies-in-waiting...'

The Fire Wielder pointed to Gemma, then very clearly and slowly he said, 'I wish to be attended by *that* young lady. I do not *want* anyone else. I would like interesting conversation until Her Majesty arrives, not stuffy court pleasantries. Oh, and please bring us two glasses of lemonade and a plate of Cook's best cakes.'

Gemma wondered who this Royal Fire Wielder could be. He obviously wasn't the sort of person one argued with.

'Immediately sir.' The butler strode back down the corridor, giving Gemma a deadly scowl as he passed.

She stared hard at the floor, trying not to giggle, but she wished the Fire Wielder had not made a fuss. She now had a new enemy in the palace.

The tap-tap of echoing footsteps bought Gemma back to reality. The strange visitor was waddling away down the corridor.

Gemma wriggled from her hiding place and followed him sedately. As they reached the library, she jumped forward to open the door wide with a flourish, just as the chief parlour maid did.

At that moment there was a terrific crash from below stairs.

'*YOWL!*' Fleabag squealed.

'I'll kill you!' the butler bellowed.

Gemma permitted herself a little grin. She could tell by the cat's voice that he wasn't really hurt.

He'd merely laid a successful ambush.

The library was a bright room lined with oak bookcases and panelled walls. Tiny specks of dust floated lazily in the golden morning sunshine as it streamed in through the open windows. The rich scent of beeswax polish mingled with the perfume from a bowl of roses.

The Fire Wielder sat down heavily in a big leather armchair and motioned to Gemma. 'Pull up a stool.'

She shook her head. 'I won't be allowed to sit in the presence of visitors, sir.'

The Fire Wielder leaned forward. His warm smile was quite startling against his conker-brown face. 'Then let us say... that I am not a visitor, but a long lost friend?'

Gemma curtseyed nervously and positioned the stool so it was opposite the little man.

Leaning back in his chair, he closed his eyes as if he

16

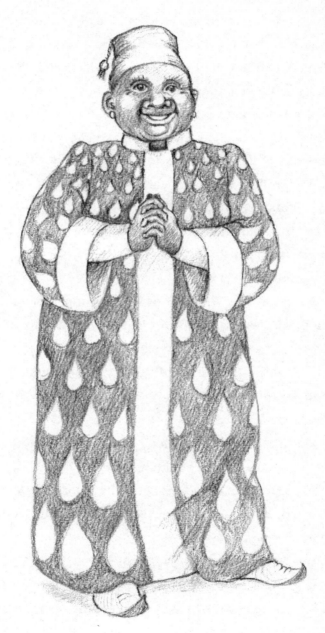

were very hot and tired. After a few moments, he pulled off his fez and ran his fingers through his grizzled hair until it stuck out at all angles. Bushy black eyebrows and a long, hooked nose gave him an air of solemnity despite his smile lines.

He tugged at his heavy red and yellow robes that glistened with too much gold embroidery. 'Forgive me,' he smiled. 'I am unbearably hot. I am supposed to wear all this stuff, but I hate it.'

He winked, then smiled. 'Now, tell me, what is your name?'

'Gemma, sir.'

'A good name. Now, let us see how much Ring Fire is in this little Gem, shall we? When I opened my hand to you by the front door, what did you see?'

Gemma's mind ran wildly, trying to imagine what could be the right answer to such a question. In the end she swallowed hard and said, 'A tiny flame, sir. A bit like the one in the queen's Ring.' She glanced up nervously. Was that what he wanted to hear?

The old man nodded thoughtfully. 'Good.'

Just then, someone knocked. A maid entered and gave Gemma a withering glare as she placed lemonade and cakes on a side table,

'Begging your pardon for interrupting, sir,' she said, 'Her Majesty conveys her deepest respects and says she'll will be with you directly.'

The maid hesitated, still staring at Gemma.

'That will be all, thank you,' said the Fire Wielder.

The woman was obviously bursting to know what was going on, but she had to leave. When her footsteps had retreated along the corridor, the Fire Wielder turned back to Gemma.

'Now where were we? Ah yes, you saw fire, did you? Like this?' He opened his hand again – but there was nothing there.

Gemma was confused. 'No, sir.'

'Good.' He smiled with intense satisfaction. 'Now, time for something to eat and drink. Tuck in.'

And they both began to eat. For a long while, their mouths were too full of whipped cream and chocolate topping to talk, so Gemma tried to think.

What did she know about the Royal Fire Wielder? What had she been taught about this strange Fire?

Nothing.

Was he a sort of king, or maybe a magician? She thought of the jugglers at the Midwinter Festival and the fire-eaters in the marketplace.

The queen had said he wasn't like any of them, yet he *felt* very mysterious.

Most unnerving of all, was the way he seemed almost to recognize her. *How*?

The little man cut across her thoughts. 'You say you have seen my Fire before?'

Gemma coughed as some cake went down the wrong way. Her mind raced. What had she said?

He sensed her anxiety and tried to help. 'You said my little flame was like the Fire in the queen's Ring?'

'Yes sir. I bring Her Majesty morning tea, and while I wait for her to wake up, I sometimes sit and look at her Ring. I…' She panicked. How could she tell him?

'Go on,' the Fire Wielder coaxed.

Gemma took a deep breath then blurted out, 'I sometimes see things in it!'

There, she thought, *now I'll be sacked for sure. What must he think of me?*

But instead of getting angry, the Fire Wielder settled back in his armchair, laced his hands over his ample stomach and closed his eyes. 'Ah!' he murmured softly.

And that was how Queen Sophia found the pair of them: Gemma was sitting bolt upright staring in confusion at the Fire Wielder, and he was leaning back in his chair, eyes closed and smiling.

The queen's silk robes rustled.

Gemma sprang to her feet, blushed, made her best curtsey and scurried towards the door.

The Fire Wielder opened one eye and reached out

towards her. 'Don't go.' Then he heaved himself out of his chair and stood before the queen.

But he did not bow.

Instead, it was she who slowly and stiffly knelt before *him*. 'My Lord Fire Wielder,' she said.

'Sophia, my dear lady!' he replied, offering his hand to be kissed before helping her to her feet and gathering her in a big hug.

4 Learn to Eavesdrop!

'Stand by the door, Gemma. We are not to be disturbed. If anyone knocks, send them away.'

Gemma's legs shook as she took her post. A soft thud at the window announced the arrival of Fleabag who then settled himself comfortably across her feet.

The warmth of the summer morning was filled with the soft murmurings of the old friends settled in their chairs, holding hands and talking intensely.

Gemma rested her head against the doorpost and closed her eyes. She had almost drifted off to sleep when one of Fleabag's well sharpened claws picked at her leg.

'Ow!' she gasped.

The cat glared up at her. She bent down to push him away, but he sprang into her arms 'Get down!' she whispered. 'I can't cuddle you now.'

But he clung on and settled himself under her chin. 'Wake up, you duff-head,' he growled in her ear. 'This involves you!'

'What?'

'Eavesdrop, can't you? You really must develop the knack, you know.'

22

'I can't do that, you wicked cat,' Gemma scolded. 'How could you even *think* of such a thing?'

Fleabag sighed. 'Why do you think they told you to stay *inside* the room? If they didn't want you to hear, they'd have put you *outside,* or even better, sent you away completely. They're talking quietly so no one *else* can hear. Now wake up, you silly furball, and listen!'

Slipping to the floor, he miaowed to be let out.

As Gemma opened the door, she glimpsed the butler with his ear to the keyhole. She pretended she had seen nothing, but smiled at the yowl and crash that followed.

Clever Fleabag, she thought.

When all was quiet once more, Gemma concentrated on the conversation between the queen and her visitor.

As Sophia's head bent forward, the sun glinted on her coronet and dazzled in the emeralds at her throat. She looked very beautiful, yet her words were chilling.

'I feel in my bones that there's much evil and injustice in my kingdom,' the queen said. 'But I am too old and tired to do anything about it. I wish for nothing more than to sleep the Long Sleep and leave all of this to someone stronger.'

She squeezed the Fire Wielder's fingers. 'But I

cannot let go until I am sure of my successor. There is no one in all my court that I can hand my Ring and my crown to. There are many wise and good people, but the Ring grasps my finger with the same firmness as the day you placed it there. It isn't ready to go to another. I do not know what to do.'

With a sinking heart, Gemma realised her beloved queen was crying.

The Fire Wielder stroked her hand. 'I know,' he said softly. 'And you are right to trust the Ring. Now, tell me about this festival of yours.'

The queen sighed. 'Hyrald, my Prime Minister, suggested it. He thought if everyone in the kingdom had the chance to say, in his or her own way, what it means to be monarch then we might find my successor. It wasn't such a bad idea...'

'But it has yielded no one?' ventured the Fire Wielder.

'No.' The queen sighed. 'That is why I have been begging you to come. I needed you.'

'I waited because I had to know what to say.'

'Even your presence would have comforted me.'

The Fire Wielder shook his head sadly. 'I may have spoken words which were not yet ripe.'

'And are your words ripe now?'

The old man looked out of the window at the rose

garden. 'Firstly, you must know that I too am tired and ready for the Long Sleep. My heart is not strong, and I think when you surrender your Ring, I will follow you quickly into the Quiet Place. But I too must find a successor. So listen to what I suggest, and tell me if it sounds like true Fire Speech.'

At his words, warmth tingled down Gemma's spine. There was something very good and *right* about the Fire Wielder, but what he was saying scared her.

'You must place your Ring into my hands...' he began.

Without hesitation, the queen tugged at the jewel, but the old man laid his fingers over hers. 'Not yet, hear me out and be certain you agree. Tonight we will perform the rite of severance and remove the Fire from the Ring. The flame will remain at the palace, for all to see, and I will send the Ring to be hidden where only a true king or a queen would dare to look for it.'

'Can the Fire survive without the Ring?' the queen asked.

'As you know, my dear Sophia, the Fire is not from this world. It will fade quickly unless it is welcome, so I will *hold* the Fire. It will burn without the Ring, but only for a year and a day.

'In that time, your subjects high or low-born, young and old, may search for the Ring and whoever finds it and brings it here may prove to be the new ruler of our land. If the wrong person finds it by accident, or if a rogue or villain takes it by force, the Fire will not acknowledge them. If the Fire welcomes the Ring-holder – then that person will be crowned.'

'But... if it fades?' The queen frowned.

'They will be sent away and we will wait for the Ring Fire to show us the way once more.'

Both were silent for a very long time.

By the door, Gemma's eyes opened wide. Were such things possible?

At last the queen said, 'It is a terrible risk, my lord.'

The Fire Wielder looked earnestly into her face. 'But is it a wise risk, my lady? Is it the *right* one?'

The queen sank back into her chair and closed her eyes. At last she said, 'When the moment comes to perform the rite of severance, if the Fire burns brightly, let us proceed. If it wavers, then let us wait. The Fire will make its choice clear in the end.'

The old man smiled. 'Such were my thoughts too.'

Just then, Fleabag reappeared on the windowsill. He leaped inside and sat by the queen's feet. She laughed and patted the arm of her chair. 'You may sit beside me, but don't you dare touch my best frock, cat,' she said playfully. 'I suppose you've been listening, you wicked animal?'

Fleabag said nothing as he sprang up next to his mistress, but he purred delightedly as she scratched behind his ear.

'Now, listen, you old rogue,' she began, 'I have an important job for you.'

Fleabag stopped purring and sat to attention, his eyes wide and golden.

'I know you understand every word I say and I'm sure you repeat everything to your disreputable cronies below stairs. But this is a secret. I want you to look after Gemma over there. She will have a difficult time ahead and two heads are better than one, even if yours is filled with furry nonsense and fish scraps. Will you care for a mere human, old friend?'

Fleabag jumped down and strode over to Gemma. He sat by her feet staring at her until she picked him up. But there were no claws this time. Just velvet paws and a rich, rolling purr.

Gemma looked at the queen in astonishment.

The Fire Wielder beckoned. 'Put the cat down and give me your hand,' he said.

Gemma did so. For a few seconds, the Fire Wielder laid his palm across hers. When he took it away, she jumped, for burning brightly in the hollow of her palm was a tiny flicker of flame.

It didn't hurt. It tingled warmly, making her glow

with happiness.

Then it was gone and she felt lost and alone.

'Whatever happens, you must remember that little flame,' the Fire Wielder warned.

Then he sighed deeply. 'Now Gemma, please ask the butler to fetch the Prime Minister. We have much to do before nightfall.'

5 The Ring and the Fire

'*Come on!*' Fleabag moaned, padding up the servants' staircase. 'Hurry, *we've* got lots to do as well.'

Gemma stayed at the bottom. 'But I can't, I've got to work. Cook'll murder me – I haven't been in the kitchen all morning.'

'Tough!' growled the cat. 'Up here. *Now.*'

Gemma sighed and ran after him.

Up in the servants' dormitory, Fleabag sprang onto Gemma's bed and clawed at her blankets. He twitched his whiskers. 'Let's get this straight. You're never going back to the kitchen, so start packing. Not much, just essentials. You don't want to be slowed down by *stuff.* Mind you,' he muttered, 'I don't see why humans need luggage anyway. Look at us cats – immaculately dressed for every occasion.' Fleabag struck what he hoped was an artistic pose.

'Were you travelling light when you forgot to pack your fourth leg?' teased Gemma.

The cat bristled his fur and turned his back. 'We've no time for silly banter,' he replied haughtily. 'Just do as you're told, please.'

'But where're we going?' she asked. 'What should I take?'

'Oh, do stop pestering me with stupid questions,' Fleabag snapped. 'It'll all come clear in good time. Just put your all things together and make sure you're in the throne room at sunset. There's going to be a proclamation. Get there early, for the rest of the world will be there too. Now, leave me in peace, I need a nap. You don't know what a hard life it is, being a cat.' And with that, he curled up, and went to sleep.

Gemma glared at him, but what could she do? An earthquake wouldn't shift him until he was ready to wake up.

In the end, she shrugged and looked around for things to pack. She didn't have much. When she'd arrived at the palace, she only had the rags she was wearing and they were burned. She'd been given two brown kitchen dresses and someone's cast-off red skirt and white blouse for holidays.

Well, she'd probably never be allowed to work here again, so she changed into her holiday things. Using her cloak, she made a bundle of her underclothes, a nightdress, two handkerchiefs and a hairbrush.

Just as she was tying a knot to secure it all, she heard, someone yelling 'Gemma? Gem-MA!'

Footsteps thundered up the wooden stairs, the

door flew open and there stood an under-chambermaid, red-faced and furious.

'Why aren't you in uniform?' she screeched and, without giving Gemma a chance to explain, she pushed her out of the door and back down the stairs.

'I've been looking for you all over the place – what do you think you're playing at?' the woman moaned, shoving Gemma in the back. 'I've got all out of puff looking for a good for nothing guttersnipe!'

She hardly paused for breath, as she steered Gemma this way and that until they were standing outside the royal bedchamber.

'Can't think what she wants to see *you* for!' the maid sneered then stormed off down the corridor.

Gemma took a deep breath, knocked and went in.

The queen was sitting alone in the room. Her jewels were put away and her grey hair hung loose over her shoulders. Her eyes were damp and red, but she smiled as the door opened.

'Sorry I took so long, ma'am,' Gemma said, bobbing a curtsey.

The queen shook her head. 'Please don't worry. There will be time for everything, I am sure. Now please help me change. I won't need these robes of state any more. Find me something light and simple.'

Gemma unfastened the queen's robes and helped

the old lady step free from their thick folds. As she slid a linen dress over the old lady's head and wrapped her in a pink shawl, she seemed to be 'Her Majesty' no longer, but more like a loving granny.

Gemma had always longed for a granny of her own. She couldn't help it – she sniffed and began to cry.

With damp eyes, Sophia put her arms around Gemma and stroked her hair. 'My dear, we will not talk again. I am going to my Long Sleep. Come and sit next to me on the bed and listen very carefully.'

They sat down together and the queen took Gemma's hands. 'Now, you heard my Lord Fire Wielder and me making plans this morning? Good. I want you to join this quest.'

Gemma's eyes opened wide. *'Me*, your Majesty? I'd do anything for you, but what use can *I* be?'

The queen looked serious. 'Because you have studied my Ring more than any of my subjects. Do you know why I picked *you* from the street when there are so many urchins who need homes?'

Gemma shook her head. 'No, I never understood.'

'It was because I saw you looking into my Ring as I helped pick you up after the accident,' the queen explained. 'You weren't looking *at* it, as everyone else does, but *into* it. I knew we would need each other one day. Since then I have often watched you staring into the depths of the stone, while you thought I slept.'

Gemma blushed. 'I'm sorry...'

The queen shook her head. 'No, I am glad you did. You are the one person I can trust to know the true Ring when you see it. Will you go? For me?'

Gemma swallowed hard. She felt very small and particularly useless. 'Ma'am, I... I'm not sure... but for you, yes, I will.'

The queen smiled and patted Gemma's hand. 'Good, and will you look after my cat Fleabag, too? He lost his leg in a great act of heroism and he holds a noble title and a great name. But it is more than my life is worth to tell you, so never let on you know.'

Then the queen leaned close and whispered in Gemma's ear, 'you probably won't believe this... but Fleabag is a *talking* cat!'

'Yes, ma'am,' Gemma replied, trying not to giggle.

The queen straightened herself and sighed. 'I would very much like to give you a parting gift, but I fear if anyone saw you with a jewels or gold, they'd not believe I had given it. They might even imprison you for theft.'

Then she smiled. 'Have my shawl, child. Your clothes are hardly fit for a journey.' She looked Gemma up and down. 'Your feet are almost the same size as mine, take the walking shoes and socks from my cupboard and fetch me another wrap please. Any one, it doesn't matter what I wear now. My part is over.'

Gemma tried to swallow the lump that ached in her throat. She tucked a blue stole around the queen's shoulders, then she dressed herself in her new things.

Leaning on Gemma's arm, the old lady rose shakily to her feet. 'Now take me into the Hall of Light where the Royal Fire Wielder is waiting. There we will say farewell.'

Gemma's voice was stuck, so she just nodded.

As they walked slowly down the long corridors, Gemma held the queen's arm. With every step, age and tiredness seemed to descend upon the old lady.

At the final turn, Gemma glimpsed Fleabag.

As his mistress entered the Hall of Light for the last time, he rubbed his fur against the queen's legs. She bent down and scratched behind his ragged ear. He purred and licked her hand, then she stood up straight.

Letting go of Gemma's hand, Queen Sophia entered the Hall alone. A footman shut the door in Gemma's face.

As she turned away, a sharp claw in her leg made

her look down. 'Go and get your bundle,' hissed the cat. 'It'll be sunset soon. Meet me in the throne room.'

Ten minutes later, Gemma returned to the throne room. Hoping no one would stop her and give her a job to do, she dodged between the palace staff arranging chairs and wheeling trolleys laden with food. At last she spotted Fleabag's tail poking out under a tablecloth.

She couldn't resist giving it a tweak. 'I'm here, she whispered.'

'Watch your manners!' Fleabag growled, then he led her to a carved pillar where they hid and watched the dignitaries thronging to their places.

'What's going to happen?' Gemma whispered, stroking Fleabag's ears.

'Sssh!' he hissed. 'You'll see,'

On all sides, the crowd buzzed with subdued excitement. Everyone knew there was about to be a momentous announcement, but no one knew what.

Gemma stood on tiptoe, trying to peer between the courtiers' fancy hats to see the queen – but she could see no further than the plumed helmets of the Queen's Guard.

Everyone was dressed in glittering robes; the room was aglow with dazzling silks, the gleam of polished swords and gold embroidery.

'I can't see a thing,' moaned Fleabag, jumping into Gemma's arms.

'Neither can I, and I've got cramp.' She rubbed her leg. 'I'm going to try and find a better place.'

Just then a trumpet fanfare greeted the arrival of the Royal Fire Wielder. Looking more comfortable at last in a loose white shirt and trousers, he stepped onto the dais and stood by the empty throne. The queen was carried in on a litter, now too weak to rise, but she greeted the people with a lift of her hand.

Hats were doffed and the company bowed. Silks rustled, lace drifted and leather creaked, then the courtiers took their seats, whispering excitedly.

The Royal Fire Wielder raised his hands for silence.

'My lords and ladies,' he bowed to left and right. 'Today, Queen Sophia has surrendered the Ring of the Kingdom. Tomorrow, she will go to her Long Sleep in the Quiet Place.'

He paused to allow the murmur of concern and protest to die down, then he continued. 'I too am ready to sleep, but neither of our successors have been found. To this end, today, in the Hall of Light, I performed the Rite of Severance.

'This Ring,' he announced, holding the jewel high for everyone to see, 'is now quite simply a plain opal

36

on a gold band.'

He paused, then added, 'And the Fire resides with me.' As he spoke, he held his other arm high and opened his hand. A golden tongue of flame blazed high into the gold and white domed ceiling.

Everyone in the throne room gasped.

A tangle of joy, recognition and fear danced

through Gemma. She clutched Fleabag so hard he scratched and struggled.

The Fire Wielder closed his fingers, and the light was gone.

'The Ring will be sent by secret messengers to a place where only the true successor to our great queen will dare to find it,' he continued. 'I will hold the sacred Fire here, in the Hall of Light, until the Ring is found and returned. When the two are truly reunited, the next queen or king will be known. Tomorrow, all those who wish, noble, servant or farmer, may commence the search. If the Fire and the Ring are not brought together within a year and a day, the Fire will fade and slip back to the place from whence it came, and then we will have to carry on without wisdom or guidance.'

At this, the Royal Fire Wielder turned and walked out of the room, followed by the queen and her bearers. Silence hung heavily as the listeners shook their heads. One by one, the people drifted away, murmuring softly.

Once the room was empty, Fleabag gave Gemma's hand a rough lick. 'Time to go, but first things first: let's eat – the food's hardly been touched!'

To Gemma's horror the cat jumped up onto the table and attacked a whole stuffed salmon. 'Come on,' he spluttered with his mouth full. 'This is good. Fill up and take some for tomorrow. You don't know when you'll eat again.'

Gemma filled her pockets with dried fruit, and pushed bread and cheese into the end of her bundle.

'Oi!' yelled a footman. '*Out!*'

With a flick of his tail, Fleabag leaped to the floor and sprang along the corridor with something large and heavy in his teeth.

At last they reached the little back stairs behind the kitchen where they had often sat and talked. No one was about. A few more steps brought them to the boot cupboard where they wedged themselves between the boxes of polish and shoelaces.

'Ere, ake is,' Fleabag mumbled.

'What?'

Fleabag dumped his loot at Gemma's feet. 'I *said*, "Here, take this."'

'A whole chicken!' Gemma gasped, grabbing it.

'Waste not, want not,' grinned the cat. 'Wings or breast?'

6 The Hall of Light

Squashed between the riding boots and the tennis shoes, Gemma couldn't get comfortable. She nudged Fleabag with her toe. 'Are you asleep?'

'I *was*,' he muttered resentfully.

'I'm tired and cold, but I daren't go upstairs to bed,' she complained. 'You're all right, you can snooze anywhere.'

'Not with you poking at my ribs, I can't,' Fleabag huffed.

Gemma ignored him. 'I'm scared. I've got to get out of here. Cook'll kill me if he catches me here in the morning. I don't know where to go – or what to do.'

Fleabag licked his ruffled fur. 'I thought humans were supposed to be the clever ones. You're asking *me?*'

Gemma leaned her head on the blacking box and stared out of the tiny window at the starlit sky.

The cat jumped onto her lap, purring loudly, then he rolled over and stretched until he almost fell off. 'I know what *I'd* do,' he said in an upside-downy sort of a voice. 'I'd go and ask the Fire Wielder.' Then with a final twist he landed on the floor and strode back into the kitchen.

Gemma didn't move.

'Well, aren't you coming? The Fire Wielder said he'd be in the Hall of Light. I don't see why you shouldn't talk to him. He was very nice to you earlier.'

Gemma brushed Fleabag's hair off her skirt. 'I'm coming.' She followed him to the servants' stair, but half way up she stopped. 'Are you sure this is a good idea?'

'I can't think of anything else to do, can you?'

Gemma thought for a minute. 'No.' Then, 'You are coming in with me, aren't you?'

Fleabag hesitated.

Gemma caught up with him and stroked his head. 'A cat may look at a king.'

'But may I look at a Fire Wielder? He might singe my fur off!'

'But you've seen him before...'

'Not when he was actually Wielding Fire,' teased the cat.

Gemma froze. She'd never thought of what the strange little man might actually *do*. The queen had said he wasn't a juggler, but how else would he wield fire?

They reached the Hall's carved doors. Gemma

touched the handle and looked back at her only friend. 'Should we be scared?' she asked. 'He did seem kind.'

Fleabag slipped away into the dark shadows. From there his rolling, laughing purr sang out, 'No, I'm not scared. It's just that it's something *you* have to do. Not me.'

Gemma leaned against the door. The cool wood calmed her racing brain. 'You're right,' she said at last. 'I've got to talk to him.' Then, with a small but determined push, she entered the Hall of Light.

The circular room was quite silent and almost dark with grey and purple shadows painting the walls. High in the ceiling, a wide glass dome showed a star-lit, indigo sky with a crescent moon.

Gemma walked forward, then stayed quite still until her eyes adjusted to the gloom. After a while, she noticed a tiny, flickering light in the centre. She moved towards it softly.

'Fire Wielder?' she whispered. 'Is that you?'

There was no answer, but the silence seemed full and alive; it did not feel like an empty room.

She took a few more steps until she was standing by a low table. The flame danced just above it.

Should she be here? Would she get into trouble?

Her heart pounded as she called out again, 'Fire Wielder, if you're here, help me please. I don't know where to go, or what to do. In all the world I've only got Fleabag – the cat. Do you remember him? Oh I wish you were here. Could you come with us to find the Ring? You'd make sure it went to the right person.'

Something creaked and huffed in the darkness.

Gemma jumped.

A round shape peeled itself from the shadows and the Fire Wielder shuffled towards the flame until his kindly face was lit by the gleam of light.

'My little Gem,' he said gently. 'I'm sorry, I was asleep.'

Gemma wished she hadn't come. She wanted to run and find Fleabag and disappear into the night. She'd go back to the alley behind the market where she used to live. What business did she have here?

She turned to run, but the Fire Wielder caught her hand. 'Ask whatever you need to know. Look steadily into the flame and be sure the Fire Giver will speak.'

Gemma turned to the flame and became transfixed. She could not move. Once again she was flooded with intense happiness and terrible sorrow, all at once.

She took a deep breath, then whispered, 'Where do I go now? What do I do?'

And into her head came the words, *Go north by northwest.*

'Who said that?' Gemma gasped.

The Fire Wielder smiled. 'The Ring Fire spoke to you.'

Gemma screamed and bolted towards a crack of light she hoped was the door... Only to collide with a very solid figure barring her way.

Leather-clad hands grabbed at Gemma. Cold chain mail pressed into her cheek. There was no escape.

'What shall I do with this intruder, my Lord?' asked a woman's voice. 'Shall she be horsewhipped?'

'Certainly not!' came the Fire Wielder's indignant reply. 'Take her to an inn, feed her and make sure she gets a good night's sleep. In the morning, you must listen to her story. She has much that will be useful to you. Remember that even guttersnipes are important in the eyes of the Fire Giver.'

'Very good, my Lord,' the woman replied.

'And above all,' the Fire Wielder continued, 'remember you are sworn to defend *all* her people, high *or* low-born, washed or unwashed. Kings and queens may disguise themselves in rags to see how their servants treat their subjects.'

'Yes my Lord.' Gemma's captor bowed and turned to go.

44

But the Fire Wielder hadn't finished. 'Oh, and one last thing, my Lady-Knight Rowanne de Montiland, please put your charge down gently, then shake hands with Gemma Streetchild. Gemma, I give you the Lady Rowanne, your protector.' He yawned. 'Now, I need to sleep.'

And with that, he shuffled back to his couch.

Rowanne scooped Gemma over her shoulder, marched her out of the hall and into the echoing, torch-lit corridor.

Twist and turn as she might, Gemma could only see her captor's silk-embroidered tabard showing the royal arms.

At last, Gemma was unceremoniously dumped by a side door. 'Out!' the knight ordered.

'I need my bundle, it's in the kitchen,' Gemma begged.

'Hurry then,' her captor grunted.

As Gemma returned, the lady-knight grabbed her and propelled her across the courtyard. As they reached the gates, the duty soldier saluted the knight, but barred Gemma's way.

'Servants' gate is at the back.'

'I'm on an errand,' Gemma replied quickly. 'It's important.'

'Don't give me none of your lies! Brat!' The man swung his arm to box her ear.

The lady-knight caught his wrist. 'She's telling the truth, Gordik. I'm to make sure she comes to no harm.'

The man shook himself free. 'Funny messenger.'

'The ways of the Fire Wielder are not to be questioned,' the woman replied tersely.

Gordik shrugged. 'Humph. Very well. Pass.' He strode back to warm his hands by his brazier.

A few minutes later, a third, smaller shadow left the palace, running with a strange hopping motion. Ignoring Gordik's offer of a meat scrap, Fleabag darted away into the dark city night.

7   The Queen's Cat

In the oak-panelled comfort of the Moon Inn, the Lady-Knight Rowanne de Montiland removed her helmet, tabard and chain mail. Even without her armour, her Ladyship could never pass as an ordinary woman. Her dark hair was coiled to frame high cheekbones and a strong jaw. She was haughtily beautiful.

Gemma guessed the Fire Wielder's commands would be carried out to the letter. After that she'd be on her own.

Fleabag slid under the table, curling himself comfortingly around Gemma's feet. His eyes were closed, but he was listening to every word.

The knight slammed a plate of bread and meat on the table, then poured two tankards of ginger ale. 'So... what have you to tell me, guttersnipe?'

Gemma sipped at her drink, but having shared a chicken with Fleabag, she wasn't hungry.

When that woman isn't looking, she decided, *I'll slip that food into my bundle for tomorrow.*

'Hurry up, I'm waiting!' Rowanne de Montiland

crossed her arms and scowled.

Gemma gulped. 'What do you want to know, my lady?'

'Whatever you have to tell. The most noble Fire Wielder told me you have important information for me. Why else do you think I've wasted good money on your bed and supper? Now tell me quickly before I return you to Gordik and his friends.'

'But what sort of information my lady?'

Pushing her ale aside, the knight grabbed Gemma and dragged her across the table until their faces almost touched. '*You* tell *me*...'

Gemma's eyes widened. 'I – I really don't know what to say. If I knew, I'd tell you. You have indeed been most generous...'

At that moment, Fleabag leapt onto the table and sat right in front of Lady Rowanne's nose.

With a most unknightly squeal, she dropped Gemma and knocked her drink flying. In one hand she grabbed her stool and with the other she drew her sword.

'Cats!' she screamed. 'Someone's let a cat in here!'

Fleabag bristled his tail. 'Snobs!' he squealed. 'Someone's let a snob in here!'

'It *talks*!' the knight wailed, bringing three of the most burly men in the bar to her rescue.

Gemma crumpled into a heap, giggling helplessly.

The men, who thought they were rescuing a damsel in distress, roared with laughter when they realized the lady-knight was scared of a cat.

Puce with rage, Rowanne snatched up their things. 'Up! *Now!*' she yelled and stormed off to their room.

Ahead of them strode the black shadow of the noble Fleabag. His head was high, his tail erect and his stride strong and brave.

At the bedroom door, lady Rowanne pointed the naked blade of her sword at the threshold. 'Come one paw stride nearer, puss, and by all I hold precious, I will have your fur for a collar.'

'No, you won't,' Fleabag replied coolly. 'I've got fleas.'

The knight touched the blade under his chin. With a sharp twist, she brought his head round until his golden eyes met her dangerous blue scowl. Neither blinked.

'Cat,' she said icily, 'I dislike cats of any description, unless they are fighting toms, on whom I might have a bet. I concede such a wager won me my velvet cloak. But unless you *are* such an animal,' she ran the shining blade along Fleabag's back, 'which, after consideration, I doubt, then fleas or not, I will have you dead at my feet unless you remove yourself

NOW.'

Fleabag did not move a whisker.

Rowanne lunged.

The cat jumped.

The sword pierced only the air where his fourth leg should have been.

'Missed!' he sang gleefully. Then with one bound he leaped onto the high beam above the doorframe. From there he could survey his new-found enemy more clearly. 'Guess what?' he spat, 'I don't like snobs much either. Not even fighting snobs. And what's more,' he hissed, 'I grew my own cloak. I didn't have to win it with a silly bet.

'Now...' He jumped to the floor. 'Are we going to bed or what? We have a long day tomorrow and I am exhausted!'

Rowanne turned with disdain to Gemma. 'Take this *creature* out to the back yard, child!'

Gemma shook her head, suppressing a grin. 'I'm sorry, my lady, but I can't do that. He was the queen's cat, and I'm not sure whether he was given to me as *my* pet, or if I was given to him as *his* pet – but I think we're together.'

Fleabag preened his fur and looked smug.

Even in the dim torchlight it was easy to see that the knight was shaking with fury (or was it fear?). She spoke very slowly. 'If that... *cat* so much as enters our room, I will sleep here – on the doorstep.'

Fleabag strode up to the door and pushed with both forepaws. 'Fair enough,' he said. 'Suits me.'

And he marched inside.

8 The Paladin

Rowanne de Montiland did not sleep well. Military training had, of course, prepared her to sleep anywhere, but her umbrage at being defeated by a mere cat kept her seething all night.

As grey dawn seeped along the corridor, Rowanne was stiff all over. Very gingerly she creaked the bedroom door open. The wretched cat was curled up and fast asleep with the girl.

The second, unslept-in bed looked so inviting. She glanced at Fleabag. Not a whisker moved. If she just lay down for a few minutes she could close her eyes and ease her aching back a little…

When she woke, it was almost mid-morning. Sunlight streamed in with May warmth and Gemma was leaning over her with a tray of bread, honey and a tankard of milk.

Lady Rowanne flung back the covers in a rage. How could she have *slept*? She was meticulously disciplined and could wake or sleep as needed.

'Thanks,' she mumbled, snatching the tray and

glancing around nervously.

'Fleabag's out hunting, Miss.' Gemma tried not to giggle.

'Good,' Rowanne growled.

While she ate, Gemma tidied the room and remade both the beds with fresh sheets. It wasn't her job, but she did it well and quickly.

When she finished, Gemma curtseyed before the knight, and said, 'Thank you for your care, my lady. I would gladly tell you what you wish to know, but as I don't know what it is – I can't.'

She picked up her bundle. 'Now I must be on my way, as I really do have an urgent job to do for Her Majesty.'

Rowanne spread thick honey on her bread. 'Where are you going?'

'North by northwest.' Gemma replied promptly, adding, 'Er, do you know where that is?'

Rowanne licked the dripping sweetness from her fingers. 'Go through the Beggar's Gate and keep on that road. Why are you going that way? There's not much to interest a child along there, no fairs or entertainments for many miles.'

Gemma hesitated, fiddling with the corner of her bundle. *What should I tell her?* she wondered, *the Fire Wielder didn't say it was a secret and he did tell the lady to look after me. She'll only laugh, but then, I'll never see her again, so what does it matter?*

Squaring her shoulders, Gemma replied, 'Well… the Ring Fire told me to go that way.'

'Don't be silly, child,' scoffed the knight, then she gulped down her milk.

Gemma went very red. She pulled herself to her full height and stuck out her chin. Looking the knight straight in the eye, she stammered, 'I may be only a child to you, but to Her Majesty, I was someone fit to send on an errand. And I will do it until I succeed – or die. So there!'

She stamped her foot and ran out of the door.

Rowanne sniggered as she took another bite of bread.

But she did not enjoy her food for Fleabag jumped onto the table, right in front of his favourite enemy. 'That was ill done, ma'am,' he commented with gravity.

Rowanne did not scream this time. She merely picked the cat up by the scruff of his neck and went to the window. It was quite a long drop onto cobblestones below.

Twisting round, Fleabag sunk his claws into Rowanne's arm. 'Let *go*!' she yelled, shaking him violently.

'Fool!' The cat spat. 'You asked for Gemma's important message then you sneer when she tells you. You're not fit to be a paladin on this quest.'

Rowanne stared, then pulled him back inside and dumped him on the nearest bed. His fur was on end and his eyes glowed like carriage lamps.

'What – did – you – say?' she gasped, clutching her bleeding arm.

Hearing the noise, Gemma ventured back into the room and picked up Fleabag tenderly. 'He said I told you what you wanted to know, though I don't know what that can have been, and you're not fit to be a – a something on this quest.'

Rowanne spoke coldly and precisely. 'A paladin is a knightly companion – but on *what* quest? The one to find the queen's Ring, you mean?'

'Yes, but I don't know why,' replied Gemma unhappily. 'Her Majesty told me to. She said the Ring will be hidden where only a king or queen would dare to look and I'll be needed to recognize it when it's found. She said I have to make sure that no fakes are passed off as the real thing. When I asked the Fire Wielder where I should start, he said, "Ask the Ring Fire." So I did, and I was told, "North by northwest." So that's where I'm going.'

Gemma paused to catch her breath. She wasn't

used to making long speeches.

Rowanne's ice-blue eyes sparked under her tangle of black hair. 'The Ring Fire really spoke to you?' she asked very quietly.

Gemma shrugged. 'I don't *know*, my lady. I can't answer that. I'm just trying to do what the queen asked because I love her and I'd do anything for her. But it's all so confusing. I wish it'd all just go away!'

For a long moment, Rowanne sat quite still.

Suddenly, she thumped the table with her fist. 'Then let's prove that shabby excuse for a hearthrug wrong. I *shall* be your paladin. Let's go north by northwest together. My squire broke his leg two weeks ago, and I noticed that for a guttersnipe, you work well. If you'll come with me as my squire or maid, or whatever you choose to call yourself, I'll feed you and give you my protection on your journey.'

Clutching her bundle tightly, Gemma narrowed her eyes. 'And what about Fleabag?'

'Oh, he won't want to come. Cats never travel far from home.'

'This one does.' Fleabag padded across the floor and surveyed the knight coolly. 'And I have sworn to stay with Gemma Streetchild for as long as she needs me.'

'I also wish to stay with Fleabag,' added Gemma.

56

'Her Majesty told me to trust him. But,' she added, looking Rowanne hard in the eye, 'she never said the same about you!'

Rowanne fought her anger. The ways of the Fire Wielder were mysterious indeed! There must be something very special about this child. She was obviously telling the truth – every word – although none of it made sense.

Yet, why shouldn't she take the girl north by north-west? Her cousin Rupert had his palace there, and he was closely connected to the queen's household. Perhaps the Ring had been hidden *there*?

And what if she should succeed in finding it? There was no need to worry dear cousin Rupert about a silly old lost ring. And if the child could identify it, then her own future looked quite rosy. She'd reward the girl suitably of course, a purse of gold – or maybe silver – and a job as under-parlourmaid at the palace.

Rowanne smirked. She could see it all.

Yes, she must go on the quest herself. The Fire Wielder had hinted as much. But first she must sweet-talk the child – and get rid of that cat!

'Very well.' The knight put on her best smile. 'I will take you to find the Ring, Gemma. I'll help you and look after you, but the cat can't come. I'm sorry, but that's how it's got to be.'

'Then, no thank you. We'd rather go alone.' Gemma bobbed a curtsey, then she and Fleabag dashed out of the door and down the corridor.

Lady Rowanne's heart sank. How could the girl not be over the moon at the offer of an escort? She had to win the child's confidence.

'She won't go far on foot,' Rowanne decided. 'I'll fetch my horse from the palace and catch up with her easily.'

As she packed up her belongings, she heard people shouting and wailing in the street below. With three long strides she crossed the room and leaned out of the window.

Crowds were gathering, bare headed and weeping.

Rowanne ran downstairs to pay the innkeeper. 'What's going on, landlord?' she asked.

His eyes were red and his hands shook as he tried to count the coins. 'Tis Her Majesty, my lady. She died an hour gone. Quiet-like in her sleep, they say. The funeral's next week, but now everyone is in mourning and turmoil, for 'tis said she named no heir. 'Twill be a worrying and tumultuous time ahead, by my reckoning.'

Rowanne nodded. 'I'm sure you're right, landlord. Did you see which way the child and the cat went?'

He scratched his head, letting dandruff fall on his

shirt. 'Can't rightly say I did,' he said. I've been watching the crowds, you see, ma'am. Them's in an ugly mood and I'm worried about my windows, that's the truth of it.'

Rowanne dashed into the street. She didn't have to look far. Rushing bodies had pinned Gemma against a wall. She was hemmed in and terrified.

Using her elbows, Rowanne waded through the melee. 'Gemma! *Gemma!*' she screeched, but the roaring crowds drowned her voice. Kicking and shoving, she managed to get close.

Gemma opened her mouth in a wordless cry. Her face was wet with sweat and tears.

Just then, the crowd surged. More and more heavy bodies shoved their way towards the palace.

With all her strength, Rowanne kicked and elbowed her way through. As she reached Gemma, the girl's eyes stared wildly, her knees buckled, and she fainted. Rowanne planted her legs far apart, then bracing her arms against the wall, she made herself into a human cage over the limp child.

Despite the battering swarm that thundered along the street, the knight did not move. Something tickled her knees occasionally, but she dared not even turn her head.

It was only when she noticed that people

sometimes shouted in pain and jumped away, that Rowanne realized the tickle was Fleabag.

Squatting between her feet he scratched the legs of anyone who came too close.

Eventually the surging crowd became a trickle.

Rowanne scooped Gemma up and carried her back to their room at the inn and left Gemma sleeping off her shock.

Then, furnished with a tankard of good beer, she sat in the empty taproom and thought long and hard.

9 Round Two to Fleabag

Several hours later, Rowanne peered around the door of the darkened bedroom. The cat was sitting bolt upright on Gemma's bed.

'Erm…' Rowanne began; she really had no idea of how to be polite to a person, let alone a cat. 'Um, Mr Cat – will you look after Gemma? Don't let her go until I get back. I'm only buying supplies, I want to help – really.'

The cat stared back coldly, saying nothing.

Rowanne tried again. 'Do you think she needs a doctor?'

Fleabag yawned, stretched, turned round twice on the bed and settled down for another sleep. 'She's fine,' he mumbled from the depths of his fur. 'Get on with your shopping. I'll keep her here.'

Downstairs, the landlord was still peering nervously into the street. Rowanne held out two silver coins. His eyes lit up. 'These are for you, if the girl and the cat are here when I return.'

The man shot out his hand, but Rowanne snatched the money back. 'I said *if* they're here.' She returned the coins to her pouch and marched into the street.

It was late afternoon when Rowanne came back with her supplies. A maid followed her in, carrying a tray of stew and fresh bread. 'Put it on the table, that'll be all,' Rowanne said, and the girl left.

Gemma was just waking up. 'What's happening?' she yawned. 'What were all the crowds about? I was so frightened.'

'Her Majesty has died,' Rowanne replied, passing her a steaming bowl of stew and a chunk of bread.

'How can you just say that as if something ordinary's happened?' Gemma's voice choked.

Rowanne rolled her eyes and waved a handful of bread. 'Eat, you'll need your strength.'

Gemma pushed the stew aside. 'I'm not hungry.'

'I said *eat*!' Rowanne shouted.

'I don't want it!' Gemma snapped, and ran outside to cry in peace.

While she was gone, Fleabag helpfully polished off the left-overs, then sprang onto Gemma's bed to lick his paws and whiskers clean. He watched Rowanne bustling around with piles of clothes and equipment, then asked, 'So, *cat-hater*, what's the plan?'

The knight glared. 'Go and find Gemma, then I'll explain.'

When Gemma returned, Rowanne tossed riding trousers, a linen shirt and a squire's leather jerkin onto the bed. 'Get changed, you can't travel in a skirt.'

The clothes were loose, but sensible and comfy. Gemma folded her own things carefully and packed them into a canvas bag.

'Those people – earlier,' she asked, 'They didn't sound sad, more like they were angry – or frightened.'

Rowanne looked out of the window. 'They've nearly all gone now. The queen didn't name a successor and it's put everyone in a panic. The Prime Minister's declared a curfew at dusk to contain any trouble. I've got permission to leave – but we have to get on the move. My captain could change his mind and recall me to the palace – and that would ruin everything,' she added quietly.

Fleabag scowled at Rowanne. 'What do you mean by that?' he challenged.

The knight folded her arms and glowered. 'It means we have to get going. So Gemma, are you coming with me or not?'

Gemma felt uneasy. 'I'm not sure...' she began.

Rowanne huffed as she flung her saddlebags over her shoulder. 'Nonsense. You know what the Fire Wielder said. Now hurry *up*! It's getting late. We must get well away from here before trouble spreads.'

'What do you think, Fleabag?' Gemma asked, scratching behind his ears.

'For once, Miss Full-of-Herself is probably right,' he replied. 'We need to be on the road. Without horses and an escort, we'll be slow and in danger. Whether we like it or not, we need to do exactly as she says – *this* time,' Fleabag added quietly.

Gemma hugged her bag. 'Very well. Let's go.' Then a thought struck her, 'Fleabag *can* come, can't he?'

The knight glared at the cat, who smirked back. 'It seems I can't do much to stop him.'

As they crossed the courtyard, Gemma plucked up courage. 'Why are you doing this? You don't like Fleabag or me – we're expensive to keep, and without us you could have got out of Harflorum hours ago!'

Rowanne squirmed as two pairs of eyes burned into her. She sighed and put down her bags. 'Very well… I too have a mind to quest for the queen's Ring. Being a royal guard is very dull. I trained for adventure and fighting, not court manners and silk costumes. I persuaded my captain to let me ride across the land to see whether soldiers are needed to keep the peace in other provinces. While I'm doing that, we can search for the Ring – together.'

Rowanne went rather red. 'Let's face it,' she blurted

out, 'I need you.'

'Ahh!' said Fleabag with immense satisfaction.

'Oh,' said Gemma, with a sinking heart.

'Does my honesty offend you?' Rowanne scowled.

Gemma put down her bundle and folded her arms. 'What you're really saying is that I'm your prisoner until I can identify the real Ring for you.'

Rowanne was flustered. 'No. No, not at all. You may leave my company any time you choose.'

Fleabag bristled his black fur into a huge mane as he sprang onto Rowanne's saddlebags. 'Swear it!' he demanded.

The knight swung a well-aimed kick at his head. 'Get off, you louse-infested old hearthrug!'

Fleabag ducked and dug a claw into the bag's richly worked leather. 'Swear it!' He glowered dangerously through his whiskers. 'Swear it, or I will scratch your posh bags to bootlaces!'

Rowanne's eyes narrowed to piercing blue points. Cat and knight began another dangerous game of out-staring one another. Fleabag extended a second claw and picked delicately at Rowanne's gold-tooled family crest.

She swallowed hard. 'I swear it,' she whispered.

'Louder!' demanded the cat.

'I swear it.'

'Now bind that oath. Swear by your knighthood.'

Rowanne went pastry-white. 'I can't do that, that's the most sacred oath a knight can make!'

'Exactly!' grinned the cat, flexing a third claw.

Rowanne's eyes silently begged Gemma for support – but the girl was clutching her bag and edging nervously towards the street.

If she got away, the girl and her infernal cat could hide in some dark alleyway within seconds. There were no crowds to delay her now.

Just then, the town crier strode past, clanging his bell. 'Dusk in half an hour. Goodly folk go home,' he bellowed.

Rowanne had to decide. She swallowed hard, 'I swear by my knighthood that Gemma and Fleabag are free to leave my company at any time and place of their choosing! But,' she added quickly, 'I also swear by the same oath that I will leave their company whenever I wish to do so.'

The courtyard fell silent except for the crier's retreating warning.

'That'll do,' Fleabag announced cheerfully. He jumped down and marched into the stable. 'Come on, look lively. It's almost curfew.'

10 North by Northwest

The evening was perfect for a ride. The warm air was musty with hawthorn, and dog daisies glowed in the waning light.

But Gemma was not happy. She sat like a sack of potatoes on Mistle, the little grey pony Rowanne had bought for her. She struggled not to complain about her aching back and legs. Fleabag didn't like riding either, but at least he could jump down to stretch his paws occasionally.

They'd only been on the road for a couple of hours, before Rowanne was already regretting her vow. They were going too slowly. They had to get a move on in case the captain of the guard changed his mind and recalled her. She ground her teeth.

She had to at least try to find the Ring.

I'll give them the slip in the dark, Rowanne decided. *The child can keep the pony and the clothes. What do a few coins matter when I could become queen?*

Her horse tossed her head and whinnied. Leaning forward, Rowanne whispered in the mare's ear, 'You're right. I must be patient. I need to keep Gemma on my side.'

She glanced back at her charge. The girl looked awfully small in her riding clothes, and there was that dreaded cat padding along at the pony's heels.

'I was stupid to bring *you* along, cat,' Rowanne said out loud.

'Perhaps *we* were stupid to bring *you*,' Fleabag retorted.

Rowanne sniffed. 'I suppose you two want a rest?'

'No, my lady,' Gemma answered. 'I'll travel as long as you wish me to.'

'That's something,' she answered curtly. The moonlit road lay like a silver ribbon between the hills. 'It's a good night for travel, we'll rest at dawn.'

The more distance there was between them and the garrison at Harflorum, the happier she'd be.

As the eastern skies brightened, Rowanne drew rein and organized a camp on a woody hillside not far from the road. Gemma ate bread and cheese, wrapped herself in a blanket and fell asleep straight away.

Fleabag, who had managed to catnap on Mistle's back, offered to take the first watch.

To his surprise, Rowanne agreed, then she too closed her eyes.

Fleabag woke them when the sun was quite high. The faint sound of tack jingling had grown steadily louder. Horsemen were approaching.

Rowanne buckled on her sword and squatted silently where she could watch the road unseen.

'Why are you hiding?' Gemma whispered. 'Anyone'd think we were in danger!'

'You never know,' Rowanne replied curtly. 'I could still be sent back to Harflorum and there's always thieves about. It pays to be cautious. Now hush, they're getting closer.'

'But I thought the Captain of the Guard wanted you to go?' Gemma asked, peering through the undergrowth at the men on the road below.

Rowanne flapped her hand for silence, then after a few moments she sat back and sighed with relief. 'They're only farmers.' She gave Gemma a friendly slap on the back. 'You're right, of course. This is a perfectly legitimate mission. I'm just worried about you. You're an important young lady.'

Gemma narrowed her eyes and wondered what Rowanne was really playing at. 'Do we always have to ride in the dark?' she asked. 'I think I'd do better in daylight.'

Rowanne nodded. 'Just to begin with. Now let's break camp and set off. If you talk to anyone, don't mention the queen. Just say I'm training you as my new squire.'

Gemma squashed the blankets into a tight roll. 'I'm useless at riding. I don't think people will believe me.'

Rowanne sighed. 'Just let me do the talking. And as for you,' she pointed a threatening finger at Fleabag, 'if you value your fur, say nothing at all. A talking cat would be very popular in a circus.'

The party travelled on, keeping the morning sun at their backs as they rode steadily north by northwest. Gemma had never left the city before and found the wide-open spaces daunting.

'Are we there yet?'

'Where?' Rowanne shrugged.

'North by north west, of course,' Gemma replied.

Rowanne snorted with laughter. North by northwest isn't a *place*, it's the direction we're taking.'

Gemma went red and stared at Mistle's neck.

As they travelled, Rowanne tried to explain the rudiments of geography and orienteering, teaching Gemma how to use the sun and a stick as a compass.

But it was useless; she couldn't get the hang of it.

Rowanne hoped that they'd not meet any of her comrade knights on the road. If they questioned Gemma on her progress, it'd be obvious the child would never be a squire.

On the other hand, when it came to camp-fire

cooking, Gemma did wonders. Fleabag was an excellent hunter, although it took time to convince him that rat, vole and field mouse were not acceptable on the human menu.

Even Rowanne had to give grudging praise when he brought back a large pigeon for supper.

Gemma already knew how to pluck and gut a bird. She stuffed thyme and wild garlic into the carcass, then roasted it slowly over a low fire.

But she was amazed to learn that milk came from cows, instead of from churns at the buttery door. Unfortunately, Fleabag could not be dissuaded from helping himself from a milkmaid's pail whenever he found one unattended.

Sleeping arrangements were less successful. Rowanne wanted to avoid the inns. She was worried that anyone talking to the guileless Gemma might guess she was important and kidnap her, so they slept rough.

Gemma could not get used to always being a little cold, even on mild nights. She hated waking to find earwigs and woodlice in her blanket, or even worse, in her clothes.

But Fleabag slept anywhere and grew fat as rodents fled the haymakers and ran straight into his paws.

One morning, Rowanne seemed particularly jolly and even spared a kind word and a scratch behind the ear for Fleabag. 'My cousin's palace is on the other side of this hill,' she told them at breakfast. 'I think there's a very good chance that the queen's Ring may be there. Then we can all go home and live happily ever after.' She stretched on the grass and smiled up at the sun.

Fleabag sniffed the air and spread his whiskers. 'Nope, you're wrong. I smell trouble ahead.'

'Nonsense!' Rowanne chided. 'It's a lovely day and we'll be sleeping in feather beds by nightfall. I don't know if I'll manage to smuggle you in, hearthrug, but you usually manage to come off best anyway.'

Fleabag twitched his tail contemptuously. 'I still say that all is not well.'

Gemma looked worried. 'Are you sure?'

Fleabag rubbed his face against her hand. 'Definitely.'

'What could go wrong as long as I'm with you?' Rowanne laughed. 'If it makes you feel better, I'll keep my sword loose in the scabbard. You're probably just smelling an overfed rat which has grown to twice your size and is waiting to pounce.'

Gemma mounted Mistle. Fleabag jumped onto her saddle and made a face at Rowanne's back as he settled his paws around the pommel. But instead of curling up for a snooze, he sat erect, eyes shining and ears pricked.

'I smell several men,' he whispered to Gemma, then added, 'They stink of fear – and anger. That lady-knight is too full of herself or she'd smell it too. But stick close to her, I think we're about to see if she's as good as she says she is.'

Just then, Rowanne caught a tiny glimpse of sun reflecting on metal amongst the trees. She slowed, unsure whether it was a drawn sword or a woodsman's axe. To be on the safe side, she reached for her pointed helmet and checked the dagger at her waist.

For a moment she wondered whether to give the knife to the child. *No,* she decided. *She'll probably just burst into tears and drop it.*

The knight sat bolt upright and sniffed the air like the cat. She glanced around for side paths, but the road was bordered by a high stone wall on both sides. Either they had to turn back now and expose their backs to danger, or else go on and face it.

Rowanne kicked her mount into a trot. Gemma and Mistle did the same.

The road swung round to skirt the hill in an

easterly direction.

Just as they entered the black shade of the trees, the low morning sun caught their eyes and blinded them.

On the other side of the wall, four men were crouching behind a gap ...

Waiting.

11   Battle Cat

But Rowanne had glimpsed a movement. Drawing her sword, she braced herself.

Footsteps – to her right.

She raised her blade …

And thrust down hard.

The robber could only gurgle as blood and air gushed from his gaping wound.

More boots pounded from behind.

Rowanne wrenched her sword free from the corpse.

In that lost moment, the next man leaped up behind Rowanne, pressing cold steel to her throat.

With a flick of her wrist, she disarmed him, elbowed him in the ribs and drove his own knife under his ear.

Then Gemma screamed.

Rowanne turned.

A younger man had Fleabag by the tail, and was swinging the howling cat around his head.

Rowanne longed to let him get on with it. He was doing her a favour.

'Help him, please!' Gemma sobbed.

Rowanne slid from her horse, ducked under the cat's orbit and caught the man's body with the tip of her sword.

As he swung round, the blade slashed through his clothes, scoring across his chest and back.

He slowed, looking down in horror as his blood splashed. Then the pain registered. He crumbled to the ground and Fleabag bounded free.

With a yowling battle-cry, the noble cat pounced upon the last assailant, who was swinging a club at Gemma.

Clawing up the man's back, Fleabag sank fangs into his neck.

In agony, the robber span around. Thinking his attacker was a man with several knives, he took a hard swing with his club at head height – missing the cat completely...

And caught Rowanne's helmet with a sickening clang.

Her eyes bulged and she staggered to the ground.

The robber grabbed the horses and ran away between the trees. This was a good day's haul: two valuable animals, a well-beaten sword and two packs.

What did it matter that his neck was bleeding and the others had died? All the more for him.

When Rowanne opened her eyes, her head was pounding. She could not think why she felt so ill – she was lying in the woods on a lovely day. The birds were singing and everything was peaceful. What could possibly be wrong?

She turned her head. The world swam. By her side was something that looked like a huge cup. She touched it with shaking hands. She knew she ought to recognize it. It was metal, pointed and had a leather collar riveted to the back. What was it?

Instinctively she pushed it onto her head. It fitted. A helmet. That was it.

She reached for her sword. It was missing.

Wincing, she forced herself to sit. Everything was coming back to her.

Gemma, who'd been cowering in the shadows, crept forward. 'I think they're all gone – or dead.'

She looked at the two men Rowanne had killed and was sick. She had become used to rabbit blood but this was much worse. On the other side of the road, the younger thief lay quite still. He was alive, but bleeding badly and no danger to anyone.

Gemma knelt by Rowanne's side. 'Are you all

right?' she asked, offering a hand up.

'Ow!' Rowanne groaned. 'Give me a minute. What am I lying on?' She rolled over.

Gemma picked up a bloody dagger.

Rowanne took it. 'That's something, at least.'

Just then, Fleabag hobbled unsteadily into Rowanne's field of vision. 'Bag of mange!' she screamed, flinging the dagger at him.

It missed.

'What did you do that for?' he mewed pitifully.

'Wretched beast. If I hadn't saved your mouldy fur I'd have got them all! Out of my sight! By all I hold precious I'll kill you if I ever set eyes on you again!' Then she fell back as dizziness overcame her.

Gemma loosened Rowanne's clothing, then went to see the wounded robber. He was only a few years older than herself, not yet a full-grown man. He had a smudge of down on his chin and dark, curly hair.

Under his golden-brown skin, he was very pale. Without thinking about whether it was right to save the life of someone who had almost killed her best friend, she fetched Rowanne's dagger, ripped his shirt into strips and bound his sword-slash wounds.

When that was done, she was thirsty. They'd had water flasks in their packs, but those were long gone. She remembered a stream near the entrance to the

wood so, picking up Rowanne's helmet, she filled it with water.

Returning to the robber, Gemma wiped his face. He groaned, opened his eyes and drank, then flopped back on the ground.

Gemma knelt by Rowanne, gave her a drink and then wetting her handkerchief, she made a cold compress for the lump on the knight's head.

I'll let them both rest a little, Gemma thought. *Perhaps someone will come by and help.*

Glancing down at herself she realized her shirt was splattered with blood and mud. She went back to the stream to wash.

To her amazement, Fleabag was there, with all three paws in the water. 'I didn't think you'd like swimming,' she said, amazed.

'I don't,' he replied miserably. 'I just can't stand the taste of human blood.'

Gemma sat on the bank and stroked her friend's head. 'What are we going to do?'

Without answering, Fleabag pounced on an unsuspecting trout and munched. Then he began a careful, all-over grooming session.

Gemma waited. It was no good hurrying him.

'Well,' Fleabag said at last, 'we need to rest somewhere warm and dry tonight, then tomorrow we go on.'

'North by northwest?'

'Where else?' Fleabag replied tersely. 'Are you going to take *her*?' he hissed in Rowanne's direction. 'She thinks it's my fault she got bonked on the head. Stupid woman. I couldn't just sit and let her do all the fighting when I've plenty of perfectly good daggers and teeth. Now she's going to be more insufferable than ever.'

Gemma sighed. 'Trouble is, we need her. One of the thieves is badly wounded and we ought to get him to a doctor. I can't do that on my own. We'll give her the slip when she goes to see that cousin of hers.'

This cheered Fleabag up. 'Good idea. Now let's get moving. I'd like to be away from here as soon as possible.'

They returned to the road and found Rowanne cleaning the dagger. Seeing Fleabag, she glared and pointed the blade between his eyes.

He put his nose in the air and ignored her. 'Don't worry, Gemma,' he whispered. 'You go on; I'll follow out of sight. We'll meet up later.'

When the cat ran off, Rowanne straightened her bloodstained clothes and put the dented helmet back on her head. 'We'll send Rupert's men back for the bodies and to see to this one.'

The thief stared at her silently.

'What'll happen to him?' asked Gemma.

'Oh, he'll be hanged, I expect,' Rowanne replied, picking bits of wood and moss from her clothes.

'Ladies, I beg a favour,' the young man called weakly.

Rowanne strode over and looked down at him. She had a sort of grudging respect for anyone who could best Fleabag.

'What is it? I'm not in a very good mood thanks to you and your friends.'

'Please, lend me your dagger so I can kill myself.'

Rowanne laughed. 'You won't have long to live, never fear.'

He coughed and blood seeped though his bandages. 'I admit I deserve to die, but please, not on the gallows. If I crawl back to the woods the others won't help me – I'll be a liability. I'll die slowly. Give me the dignity of a swift death, I beg you.'

Rowanne crossed her arms and glowered. 'You're a fine one to talk of dignity, with the life you lead – or should I say, led?'

The boy tried to shrug. 'What else does an orphan lad do? My parents were unjustly put to death by that tyrant Prince Rupert. My only friends were thieves. No one else would spare me a crust.'

Rowanne bared her teeth. 'Prince Rupert is my much-loved cousin, scum.' She kicked him viciously and smiled at the bloodstain on her boot.

Gemma knelt down next to the boy. 'Will he stand trial?'

'Of course.'

'Then shouldn't he be well enough to speak in his own defence?'

'He hasn't *got* any defence,' Rowanne replied curtly.

Gemma leaped to her feet and shook her fist. 'What harm did he do you? It was Fleabag he went for!'

Rowanne grinned with delight. 'That's true. But it would have been us next. He's still a villain who deserves to swing.'

Gemma lifted her chin defiantly. 'You killed two men today; he killed none. You happen to be the Prince's cousin; he's an orphan. You're a rich villain, he's a poor one.'

Rowanne thrust her face close to Gemma's. 'You sound like that infernal cat!'

'Please, I beg you,' whispered the boy on the ground, 'by the mercy of the Fire in Her Majesty's Ring, lend me your dagger and I will be no more bother to either of you.'

At these words, Gemma and Rowanne both turned and stared at him.

Suddenly, Gemma felt that strange burning in the palms of her hands. The Fire Wielder had told her never to forget it.

She breathed deeply. She needed all her courage. She couldn't rely on Fleabag.

This was *her* battle.

Holding the tingle of the Ring Fire clearly in her mind, she curtseyed formally and bowed her head. 'My Lady Rowanne de Montiland, I thank you most humbly for your assistance both in the past and today. If you will grant me one request, I promise that both I and the cat will be out of your sight forever.'

'And what is your request?' Rowanne demanded, her face like a storm cloud.

12 The House of Aelforth

The knight and the child staggered as they helped the young thief to stand. He could hardly walk and had to rest every few minutes. On horseback, the journey would have been only half an hour, but their uneven struggle took the best part of the afternoon.

'My name is Phelan,' the thief said, between groans.

'I'm Gemma,' she replied, too tired to say more.

Rowanne scowled and kept silent. She was furious she'd been talked into helping the boy find a doctor in the city, but the thought of being free of them all forever was worth the inconvenience – or so she kept telling herself.

She carefully avoided remembering Gemma's part in finding the queen's Ring.

The city's yellow stone walls and welcoming gateway gleamed warmly in the late sunshine. The city guards did not move from where they lolled, as they watched the travellers approach.

As they crossed the drawbridge, Phelan sank to the ground. Rowanne strode up to the sergeant. 'Why didn't you run to help us, man? You could see we've got a wounded boy!'

The man laughed. 'And get peasants' blood on our uniforms? That's a good one!'

Rowanne drew herself up until she looked down on the soldier. 'I am the Lady Rowanne de Montiland, cousin to your lord, Prince Rupert. She gestured towards Gemma and Phelan. 'I defended these people who were set upon by thieves, on a road you did not see fit to patrol.' She held up her signet ring. 'Look – the de Montiland crest. Now give me assistance immediately, or I assure you my cousin will hear of this!'

The man blanched and called to his fellow. 'Fetch a horse and take m'lady to the castle. Quick!'

She leaned down and whispered to Gemma, 'You know, I don't think I really need you – I honestly doubt if you'd know the queen's Ring from a peddler's trinket. Farewell.'

Then Gemma and the young robber watched their paladin disappear between the houses, looking very pleased with herself.

The sergeant scowled at Gemma. 'I suppose you had your money pinched?'

She nodded miserably.

'And,' he added wearily, 'You don't know no-one

in the town neither?'

Gemma shook her head.

'We don't allow vagrants here. Go to the hostel for poor travellers. Down there, on the right. House with a green door.' With that, he turned back to his sniggering companions.

Gemma opened her mouth to ask if he'd help them get to the hostel, but she could see it'd be no use.

Something warm and soft pushed at her legs.

Fleabag had caught up with them.

Remembering she mustn't let anyone know he could talk, she bent down and scratched him behind the ears. She'd find a quiet place to have a heart-to-heart with him later, in private. She still had to apologize to him for saving the life of his assailant.

Fleabag sprang onto her shoulder and nuzzled his nose into her ear. 'You walk ahead. I'll see where you go and meet you later,' he whispered. Then jumping down, he disappeared into the lengthening shadows.

With a lonely sigh, Gemma helped the boy to his feet. 'I know this is going to be hard, but you'll have to walk on your own. You can lean on my shoulder, but that's all I can manage.'

The two struggled down the narrow backstreet the guard had shown them. Rubbish and mud clogged the open drain and the air stank.

The boy looked as if nothing mattered to him any more. 'Why didn't you just kill me back there? It would've been better for you and for me. You could've stayed with your mistress and slept in the palace.'

Gemma gave a short, hard laugh. 'She's not my mistress and I'd rather sleep in the gutter than be with her. We were simply going the same way. She looked after me because it suited her.'

The boy nodded. 'I've met people like that.' Laboriously they staggered on until they reached the green door. Gemma knocked, but there was no reply. She tried the handle. It was locked.

She let Phelan sink to the litter-strewn mud and tried not to cry.

Then from behind them, a husky voice asked, 'Can I help you?'

Gemma turned to see a kind-looking man with a spiky beard and a long, homespun robe. In one hand was a large bag full of vegetables and in the other, a huge iron key.

'It's a good job you came now,' he smiled, opening the door and putting his bag inside. 'Once I've collected the market leftovers, I bar the door until morning. It looks like this fellow needs a bit of help.'

The man looked at Phelan thoughtfully for a

moment, then handing Gemma his bag, he stooped down, hauled Phelan to his feet and helped him indoors.

The hostel was a low, stuffy room with straw pallets pushed closely together along both walls. Men and women in various states of sickness and poverty sat staring into space or walking up and down in a lost sort of way. One or two were sweeping or peeling potatoes.

The man put Phelan onto a spare mattress. 'Wait here,' he said.

Gemma sat on a bench and stroked Fleabag who'd managed to slip in as well.

Without speaking, the cat winked at Gemma, then jumped out through the window and disappeared.

The man returned with a bowl of water and clean rags. He knelt down by Phelan and whistled in amazement as he eased back the blood-caked rags.

'What happened?' he asked.

'We were set on by robbers on the south road, just where the hill is crowned by woods.'

'I know the place,' the man replied. 'It's notorious.'

The man seemed kind, but Gemma decided not to trust anyone without Fleabag's say-so. 'My name's Gemma,' she explained. 'I'm from the city of Harflorum. My mistress died and I took to the road because I thought the other servants would treat me badly if I stayed. I don't know this lad, but I think his name's Phelan. He just happened to be... on the same stretch of road, at the same time.'

The man shot her a sharp glance. He must have guessed what she meant. She didn't want to lie, but she had no intention of telling the truth either. Anyway, Rowanne was far guiltier than the boy. She was malicious, unfaithful and only concerned with getting the Ring for herself.

Right now, Gemma hated her.

'I've got no money,' Gemma went on, 'but I'm good at cleaning. May I work for our keep until the boy's better?'

The man sat back on his heels and glanced at her rough hands. She was telling the truth. 'Thank you,' he said. 'That's a good offer. My name is Aelforth, and I'm going to need a great deal of help in the next few days to get young Phelan here back on his feet. Now, this water contains salt and will hurt him a great deal, but I must bathe his wounds. You hold his hands so he can't struggle. With any luck, he'll stay unconscious while I do it.'

That night, Gemma lay on a scratchy little mattress and cried. Not because Rowanne had betrayed her –

she'd expected little else – but because she'd lost the soft pink shawl the queen had given her.

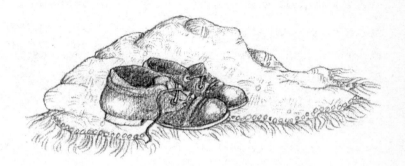

13 Rowanne Washes Up

Four days later, Fleabag sprang in through the hostel's open window. It wasn't quite light and he needed a little more beauty sleep before morning. Padding over to where Gemma slept, he arranged himself comfortably under her chin.

She moaned and struggled in her sleep. At last, she woke up and shoved him off.

'Hey!' Fleabag growled. 'I was comfy there.'

'I couldn't breathe with your tail up my nose!'

'You could've asked me to move in a friendly way.'

'Your paw was in my mouth.'

Fleabag arched his back into a big stretch, then he sat down, stood up and turned around twice. At long last he settled, face to face with Gemma.

She scratched him behind his left ear and said, 'I owe you an apology.'

'What for?'

'For rescuing Phelan after he'd swung you by the tail. I hope you're still talking to me. I had to do something. No one deserves to be left at the mercy of Prince Rupert. If only Her Majesty had known what he was like… Oh, but that's all past,' she sighed.

Fleabag licked her cheek and rolled over on his back, leaving his three legs stuck up in the air at ridiculous angles.

For a while he purred his deep, rolling song, then at last he said, 'I *was* cross at first. But what he did wasn't against me personally, was it? It was the only way he knew how to live. When I heard his story, I felt he deserved a chance to be different. I might just accidentally use his leg as a scratching post when he's well, but let's see how he turns out. If he's a decent sort, I might allow him to travel with us, but if he's a baddie then I'll feed him to a particularly unpleasant Rottweiler I met last night.'

Fleabag turned his head so Gemma could see that yet another chunk was missing from his right ear.

'Wow!' she gasped. 'Does that hurt?'

'Nah!' sneered the cat. 'Once you've had one chunk taken out of an ear, the rest is kitten play.'

But when Gemma tried to inspect the tear, he winced and presented his other ear to be stroked. 'You're a fraud,' she chided. 'Tell me if you need something on that.'

'It'll be gone tomorrow, it's only a scratch.' Then Fleabag chuckled. 'The snot-nosed mongrel I was fighting will be feeling sore this morning. He'll need a whole pot of ointment on his tail – if he's still got one. By the way, changing the subject to less interesting matters, how is Phelan?'

Gemma sat up, dislodging Fleabag who rolled onto the floor. She peered across the shadowy room. 'I can't see from here, but yesterday he wasn't being a very "patient" patient at all. Since his fever went, he keeps trying to run away. He doesn't believe we're not going to give him to the guards. He doesn't trust anyone.'

Fleabag chuckled. 'Never mind. This'll make you laugh: I've found her Ladyship Rowanne Fancypants.'

Just then, the woman on the next mattress stirred. Gemma put her fingers to her lips. 'Let me get dressed and we'll go outside. If anyone hears you talking, you'll be put in a circus.'

'I'd like to see them try!' said Fleabag, jumping onto the window sill.

The garden behind the hostel was used for growing food and hanging washing. The breeze was fresh and pleasant; it was too early for the hot city smells to clog the air.

Gemma sat in the shade of a leafy plum tree laden with tiny, unripe fruit. She hugged her knees, her eyes bright with excitement.

At her feet, Fleabag lay stretched out next to her,

his eyes closed and looking quite asleep.

In reality, he was speaking very, very quietly. 'About Rowanne,' he said, 'I have this on excellent authority. There's this bright little tortoiseshell in the kitchen. Nice lass. Could get fond of a cat like her...'

Gemma twisted Fleabag's long black fur between her toes and tugged. 'Get on with the story, mog!'

Fleabag took a friendly swipe at her toes, then settled back to the tale. 'Well, this friend of mine saw the lady-knight Rowanne de Montiland arrive at the palace gates, looking like something the dog dragged in, but pretending she was the Queen of Sheba. Apparently, she stuck her pretty little nose in the air and presented her ring to the guards, like she did at the gate...'

Gemma giggled and extended her hand, flapping her fingers. 'Like this?'

'Exactly like that!' Fleabag laughed. 'But this guard wasn't having any of it. He was a big fat man from the west, with muscles like barrels. In a blink, our friend was off her horse and thrown into prison, and I *mean* thrown – down the steps head first, so I hear. This guard reckoned Rowanne was a thief who'd stolen the ring, and had her up on a charge of imitating a member of the de Montiland family, as well as suspected murder of the real Rowanne!'

Gemma's eyes opened wide. 'But couldn't her cousin vouch for her?'

Fleabag twitched his whiskers. 'That's the best part, he's away!'

Gemma clapped her hands. 'Oh, I like it! It serves her right! When's the trial?'

'Yesterday. Some Sheriff who'd never met Rowanne sat in judgment but, because they couldn't get the ring off her finger, he thought there might be a slight possibility she's telling the truth. There's a dent in her skin that shows she's been wearing it for a long time. So, until prince Rupert returns, the Sheriff's condemned her to menial work in the kitchens. My friend says servants keep running away, so anyone they don't like, but who isn't quite bad enough for prison, is condemned to kitchen duty.'

Gemma grinned. 'Better and better!'

Fleabag purred contentedly. 'I found the scullery where Rowanne works and I sat on a window ledge where I could see it all. She was *washing up*.' Fleabag rolled on his back and purred contentedly. 'I watched her for hours. I smiled and waved a paw of course.'

'Did she see you?' Gemma's eyes were wide with delight.

Fleabag smirked. 'I made sure she did.'

'And?'

The cat ruffled his fur in disdain. 'She threw a dish mop at me. That's the last time I'll try and be friendly to her!'

Gemma lay next to Fleabag on the warm grass. 'That's excellent news,' she said. 'But right now, we have a problem. The law here says penniless travellers are only allowed to stay for one week – something to do with not wanting vagrants and beggars around the city. Aelforth says that's stupid. He gets people well and clean and almost ready to look for work, then he has to turf them out – and they can't come back for a month. After sleeping rough all that time, they're ill and dirty again.'

'Who makes the rules?'

'Prince Rupert, of course. Anyway, a sergeant comes round every day and checks the guest list, making sure the rules are followed. We're only going to be allowed to stay three more nights. Should we try and take Phelan with us? His gang won't take him back. And what do we do about Rowanne? Do we rescue her?'

Fleabag growled. 'We promised her she'd never hear from us again.'

Gemma chewed her nails. 'I suppose, like Phelan, she's a human being who needs help.'

'Call that a *human being*?' Fleabag's fur bristled.

Gemma tapped him on the head. 'Don't be nasty. To be fair, we were sort of given to each other by the Fire Wielder. I can't get rid of the feeling we're meant to stick together, it's just that Rowanne is proud and doesn't like to admit it.'

'Ummm,' Fleabag said, swiping lazily at a butterfly.

But Gemma was determined. 'I think Rowanne

ought at least to know we're here if she needs us. And that we're leaving on, let's see...' She counted her fingers, 'Thursday.'

Unconvinced, Fleabag repeated his 'Ummm,' then he twisted his head round to see Gemma properly. 'You look sort of Ring Fire-ish at times – and this is one of them.'

Gemma rubbed at the palms of her hands. They *did* tingle rather, but she didn't want to think about it. 'This window where you saw her – could I reach it and talk to her?'

Fleabag blinked his golden eyes. 'If you must.'

'Good, but you'd better keep out of sight in case she cuts another couple of legs off.'

The scullery window was barred and bolted, but a small pane was propped open so the maid could throw scraps and bones into the courtyard below. The mountain of rotting rubbish under the sill was slippery and smelled evil.

Fleabag climbed it lightly, but when a pretty tortoiseshell mewed at him from a rooftop, he waved a paw and said, 'Rowanne's in there,' and leaped away.

Nervous and sickened by the stench, Gemma clambered up the rubbish heap and peered inside. A woman was working at the sink, scrubbing pans. She was dressed in a none-too-clean peasant's dress with her black hair tied with a greasy kerchief.

Gemma knocked at the glass.

A cross face glowed back. It was Rowanne.

Gemma smiled. 'Are you all right?'

Rowanne scowled. 'No, I am *not*. No one could be all right in this hell hole.' She tossed her scrubbing brush aside and leaned on the sink. 'How did you find me?'

'Fleabag knows one of the kitchen-cats.'

Grabbing a bread knife, Rowanne waved it wildly. 'Don't mention that animal's name to me, ever!' Then she took a deep breath and calmed a little. 'Everything will be all right this evening, Rupert comes home and I'm to be brought before him.'

Then, from the kitchen came the crash of dishes and loud swearing, followed by heavy footsteps.

Rowanne flapped her hand at Gemma. 'Duck! Here comes the chief kitchen-maid. She's a fat pig and I hate her!'

Gemma squatted out of sight.

'Lazy cow!' a harsh voice screeched. 'Get that lot done before I'm back, or it'll be the horse-whip for you.' Then came the clatter of iron pots dumped on a table, and the footsteps retreated.

'All clear!' whispered Rowanne.

Gemma peered over the window-sill once more. 'Listen, I can only stay at the traveller's hostel for a few nights, then I'll be on my way again. Are you coming?'

Rowanne bit her lip and scrubbed half-heartedly at a frying pan. She'd been wrong to be so rude to Gemma. She would need her to identify the Ring. Smiling sweetly she said, 'Once Rupert recognizes me, I'm sure I could get you a job here. Why don't you stay with me?'

'No, thank you!' Gemma replied with a shudder.

Suddenly a passing soldier yelled, 'Oi you, no begging at palace windows. Move along!' He picked up a rotten potato and lobbed it at Gemma.

She slithered down the pile and ran for her life.

'I'll send for you tomorrow!' Rowanne called after her.

14 Fleabag Plays Marbles

Dinner with Prince Rupert was a grand affair at the simplest of times. Restored to her full status, Rowanne chose to wear the full court dress of a lady-knight: rose silk pantaloons and stockings, satin shoes and a white tabard with Prince Rupert's crest. Her long dark hair flowed loosely over her shoulders and smelled of lavender.

She dabbed at her pink lips with a damask serviette and nibbled at a little of the fruit set before her. She smiled as the guard who had arrested her was sentenced to ten years' hard labour.

The man was led away, howling, 'But I was doing my duty, sir! What about my wife and kiddies? Who's going to look after them?'

'Oh, very well,' yawned the prince.

The man turned with a look of relief on his face.

'Give the family ten years' hard labour as well, then they can be together.'

Rowanne closed her eyes for a second, and imagined a picture of lonely, frightened children. She winced.

Rupert inclined his head to Rowanne. Mistaking her look of horror for anger, he asked, 'My dear cousin, does that not please you? How else can I beg your forgiveness for the terrible treatment at the hands of these ill-bred, misbegotten thugs I am forced to employ!'

Rowanne laughed lightly, but a tiny scratch caught at her silken stocking. She brushed it away. 'Consider it never happened. *Dear* Rupert, it is so good to see you. I can forgive anything.'

The Prince tossed a white grape into his mouth. 'Should I have him hanged?'

Rowanne remembered the terrified thief boy looking up at her and begging not to be sent to the scaffold.

At that moment, *two* claws caught at her stocking and scratched her leg. That infernal cat!

She dropped her napkin on purpose and stared into Fleabag's accusing golden eyes. 'If you don't go away, I'll scream, and I'll have you flayed alive for clawing me!'

'No, you won't,' smirked the cat. 'You know perfectly well that a cat saved the Prince's life when he was little. The attention of a cat is considered the highest honour in this palace.

'I'll think of something,' she assured him, and he

smirked back at her.

She sat up again. 'No, don't hang the man,' she said to Rupert. She hesitated. 'It was a mistake, after all.'

The Prince lifted one eyebrow and plucked at the bunch of grapes. 'What do you suggest?'

A full set of claws tore at Rowanne's stocking. She jumped, then added, 'Er, he *was* trying to do his job. It wasn't his fault he'd never seen me before. I *was* dirty and ragged after the fight, could he not just be…'

The first set of claws on her leg was joined by more on her other leg.

She jumped again. Her voice squeaked, 'Maybe he should just lose rank and be sent back to work?' she ventured. One set of claws lessened their torture.

Prince Rupert looked amazed. 'Oh, very well,' he yawned, 'I'm tired of all this.'

The man was marched out of the room.

Rowanne smiled warmly. 'I do think your judgments are so *wise*, dear cousin.' At that moment, the second set of claws disentangled themselves, and warm fur engulfed her feet in a comforting wrap.

Fleabag purred loudly.

The Prince smiled back at Rowanne. He loved flattery. 'I'm glad you are here, I wanted to talk to you anyway. Dear cousin, I have much to discuss.'

'So have I.' She put her head on one side. She could

feel the cat bracing himself for an attack if she spoke one word out of place. Why had she let herself be bullied by him?

The purr grew louder.

'What is that noise?' asked the prince.

'Oh,' Rowanne hesitated. 'There's a... cat under the table. I was just stroking him!' At the lie a sharp claw picked at her already sore leg.

'Oh, I am so pleased,' the prince replied. 'You used not to be fond of cats. In fact, that very thing has prevented me from speaking of that which burns within my heart.'

Then to Rowanne's horror, the prince knelt at her feet and took her hand. 'Dearest cousin, will you marry me? You have been honoured by a palace cat, surely this is a sign our union was meant to be?'

Rowanne went red and white in turns. This was the last thing she'd expected. Before the queen's death, she might have said yes – but things were different now.

She gulped. 'My prince, what can I say? It is such an honour! Before I can answer you, there is something you need to know... something that may have a bearing on your request.'

He resumed his seat, but still clutched her hand. 'Speak on, my dearest. We must have no secrets if we are to be wed.'

Rowanne swallowed hard and began to tell a very edited version of what had brought her to his palace. In her story, she told how the queen herself had sent her on this mission to find the Ring. 'Think, my beloved,' her eyes were wide and urgent, 'When I find it, I will become queen of the entire land, not just princess of the province.'

'And I shall be king,' the prince breathed rapturously. 'I have heard of the quest, of course – every street corner is buzzing with the gossip. And as a relative of the late queen, I have, of course, been officially invited to take part. But it's a big undertaking. I'm still thinking about it.'

Then he sat up straight and clapped his hands.

A footman bowed. 'Your will, my lord?'

'Summon the palace jeweller,' Rupert demanded. 'And make sure he brings me every box of trinkets I possess. I wish my fiancée to choose her engagement ring.'

He winked slyly at Rowanne. 'It must be very special. I think she should have a large stone, something about the size of a robin's egg.'

He glanced at Rowanne. She gave a short nod.

Rupert smiled slowly. 'And I think we'll have... an opal,'

The poor jeweller spent long hours, deep into the night, bringing box after box of rings to his royal master. But there were very few with opals. With downcast eyes (for he feared for his neck) he informed the prince and the lady, 'There's been a bit of a run on opals since Her Majesty's death. It's funny,' he mused, 'no one seemed to like them much before.'

Time and time again he was sent back to the treasury to open more safes and to rummage through ancient chests and boxes. At last, with relief and delight, the little man presented a ring with three magnificent opals held in eagles' claws.

Rowanne still shook her head. 'I fancy,' she winked secretly at the Prince, 'one with a simple band, and perhaps just one, large opal – with a fire in it.'

The jeweller looked frightened, for he knew exactly what Rowanne meant. 'Yes m'lady.' His hands shook and his face glistened with sweat.

'I am very tired now,' yawned Rowanne, 'but in the morning, I will draw what I have in mind for you.'

The jeweller bowed. 'Very good, ma'am. A drawing will help a great deal. I will go and look through my stock of raw stones immediately, to see what can be polished and mounted for your pleasure.'

The prince waved his dismissal and the terrified man scurried away.

Rowanne smiled knowingly at the prince.

He nodded. She was clever. Very clever. He liked that. She would be very useful when he was king.

Then she rose to her feet. 'If I am to stay here, dearest, I would very much like my personal maid sent for. We were separated at the gates when the misunderstanding occurred. I have heard she is at the poor travellers' hostel. Her name is Gemma Streetchild. She is new to my service and timid, so do not send for her until the morning.'

'But of course, beloved,' Rupert replied. 'Anything your heart desires.'

Rowanne smiled. 'Thankyou. Would you mind if I went to my room now – *dearest*?'

The prince rose and kissed her hand.

As she left the room, he noticed the huge tears in her silk stockings and the trickles of blood that had ruined her new shoes. Were those *claw* marks?

Gemma Streetchild was not to be found when a servant went to the hostel in the morning. For once, even Fleabag did not know where she was.

Aelforth just shook his head. 'The people come,

and the people go. They have no homes or addresses.
When I ask them questions they have no answers.'

'I will look around, if I may?' The servant stepped
gingerly past the rows of hopeless and frail guests.

Aelforth stroked his greying beard and wondered
how he could warn the girl. The hostel would be
watched now, and he did not trust whatever was
afoot. He began his morning rounds of the sick. It was
then he realized that the boy, Phelan, was also gone.

That worried him. He had pretended he didn't
recognize the boy, but he knew all too well who he
was – and that he needed help.

Gemma had got up early to sit in the garden. As she walked through the hostel, she too had discovered that Phelan was missing.

She slipped out of the back door and climbed the garden wall. Sitting on top, she could see along the street in both directions. Cat-like she jumped down on the other side and made for the town gate. It was still bolted. She wasn't surprised, for it was scarcely dawn.

So – Phelan must still be in the city, but he had no friends or family, unless he knew some sympathetic thieves. Why had he run away when there was nothing to run away *from* and nowhere to go *to*?

She felt sad, hurt and a little lonely. She hadn't got to know Phelan well, for he hardly said anything, but she wished him no harm. He had found life tough and he had grown up having to fight all the way, but he was nice enough for all that.

And apart from Fleabag, he was her only friend.

Tomorrow she and the cat must leave the city and go north by northwest on their own. She would have been glad of someone else to talk to, someone who wouldn't sneer at her, and someone who didn't chew up dead rats for breakfast.

Slowly she wandered back to the hostel and walked straight into the arms of Rowanne's messenger. There was no use denying who she was.

110

Aelforth was not the sort of man to tell a lie.

As she went to thank Aelforth, she leaned close and whispered, 'He left very early, but I don't know where he is.' She glanced at Phelan's empty bed to show her meaning, and Aelforth nodded.

The servant had asked nothing about the boy, and both Gemma and Aelforth wanted to keep it that way.

Gemma was taken to a neat attic bedroom in Rupert's castle. As the personal maid to the prince's supposed fiancée she was given a pretty blue dress and treated almost civilly.

As soon as she had bathed and made herself presentable, Gemma was sent for. She was shown into Prince Rupert's library, where Rowanne sat at one side of a huge desk and the skinny hook-nosed prince at the other.

Gemma did not like the look of him. His eyes were narrow and hard.

Spread between them on the table were hundreds of rings. Some had opals, others had large round stones of other hues. In the corner cowered a grey little man with a huge watch-glass in his right eye. He looked like a rather moth-eaten old owl.

'My maid may not look like much,' Rowanne hesitated, the girl did look better nicely dressed, 'but she has a very good idea of the engagement ring I fancy. Come here, child.'

Gemma took one nervous step forward.

Rowanne dragged her closer and tapped a pencil and paper on the table. 'Draw! Draw me the ring I have always hankered for, *dear* girl!' She reinforced her demand with a sharp kick from under the table with her leather, cat-proof boot.

Gemma's eyes stung with tears. What could she do? She picked up the pencil. How could she make the drawing look enough like the royal ring to fool Rowanne, but not enough to betray the queen?

Just then, with a magnificent rumbling purr, Fleabag jumped on the table. With kittenish glee he patted the rings with his paws, sending them skimming across the room in cascades of glittering light.

'Oh my gold! My gems!' squealed the jeweller as he bent his rheumaticky knees and scooped the stones into numerous little bags.

At first, prince Rupert was playful with Fleabag, but then he gasped, 'Watch out! The stones are slipping between the floorboards. Oh dear! Oh *dear*!'

Rowanne paled. That cat must be got rid of! But easier said than done. Her fingers itched to do him real damage.

Fleabag didn't care. Having pounced and danced across the table, sending papers and gems everywhere in a merry scramble, he then leaped on the floor and skittishly skidded across the polished boards.

He played croquet with the crystals, and marbles with the moonstones, he bowled the blue agates, and jammed jaspers between the floor joists.

Gemma crawled under the table, pretending to help pick everything up. But once she was out of sight, she gently flicked the stones so Fleabag could pounce on them.

After several minutes of this, even Prince Rupert no longer found the cat's antics amusing – and Rowanne had found a sword. Every muscle in her body was ready to slice the cat in two.

But Rupert intervened. 'Don't kill him, my dear, he's only a poor dumb animal after all.'

Rowanne scowled at the prince, she opened her mouth, thought better of it and shut it again. She needed Rupert's goodwill. 'Take the cat away, Gemma,' she said. 'Put him in the kitchen, then come back here and clear up this mess.'

Fleabag allowed himself to be caught. Nestling contentedly in Gemma's arms, he stuck out his tongue at Rowanne as he was carried past. She bristled, but could do nothing except sheath her sword.

Gemma spent the rest of the day on her knees, gathering up loose gems and rings of every shape and size. The next day, carpenters came to take up the floor and remove the skirting boards, until every last stone was found.

Gemma drew a likeness of the Queen's Ring, but she comforted herself with the thought that the quality of stone could never be matched – and the fire was unlike anything else that had ever burned in all the world. No jeweller on earth could even begin to imitate it.

Then she smiled, for the Ring they were looking for would have no fire at all. The real Fire was safely in the Hall of Light.

But she didn't mention it.

As the days passed, Gemma found herself kept busy at the palace with no prospect of resuming her travels. She didn't mind too much. It was early summer, and a palace seemed as good a place as any to begin looking for a royal Ring.

She supervised Rowanne's extensive new wardrobe of clothes and cleaned her suite of rooms. But in her spare time, Gemma was sent out with a team of girls to 'spring-clean' the palace. Her task was to check in every nook and cranny in case, by any chance, the queen's Ring had been hidden there.

This pleased Gemma, for although she had no wish to be queen, she did want to help find the Ring – and to make sure that Rowanne did not.

Fleabag wandered around the palace at will and kept Gemma informed of all the gossip.

One day, he ran into Gemma's room and jumped on her bed. 'I've got exciting news,' he announced.

15 Gemma Speaks Out

'You remember I told you about Tabitha, the nice little tortoiseshell in the kitchen?' Fleabag rolled over the bed for Gemma to rub his tummy. 'She says that about the time the queen died, three ravens landed on the palace roof. Now she likes the tiles, does Tabitha, we've often spent a pleasant evening up there...'

Gemma gave the cat a gentle poke. 'Get on with the story, I don't care what you get up to at night.'

Fleabag twitched his whiskers. 'Well, as I was saying, Tabitha was about to catch one of the birds for supper, when she heard them talking.

'The first one said, "Here! Let's put it here. A king or queen is bound to look for a royal ring in a palace – where better to find a new sovereign for our land?"

'But the second raven shook his head and said, "No, no. True royalty lies in wisdom, not in palaces and soldiers. A king may live in a palace, but without wisdom, he is no king at all."

'It was then Tabitha saw that the third raven carried a large opal ring in its beak.

116

'She was so amazed, she slid off the ridge. The ravens heard her and flew away.'

Gemma picked Fleabag up and nuzzled his warm fur. 'Clever Tabitha and clever you!'

His whole body shook with purring.

'So, what are we going to do, cat?' she asked quietly. 'We've been here for weeks. The summer's almost gone and people are beginning to lose hope that the Ring will ever be found.'

Fleabag jumped down. 'We should've guessed it wouldn't be hidden anywhere belonging to such an unwholesome creature as Rupert.'

Gemma shuddered. 'Now Rowanne's unofficially betrothed to him, it looks like I'll be kept here all winter.'

Fleabag scratched hard. 'At least my fleas will die off when it gets cold.'

Gemma took no notice. 'The other day, the prince was talking about what'd happen if the Ring wasn't found. There was a great deal I didn't understand, something about seeing who was and wasn't fit to rule, and the prince said he'd make sure his soldiers were ready to fight. Will there be war if the Ring Fire goes away?'

'I expect so.' The cat rolled over on his back. 'Scratch my tummy again!' he demanded. 'I like it.'

Absent-mindedly Gemma did as she was told. 'Rowanne will never leave here. She has it made whatever happens next. Prince Rupert was the old queen's nephew and Rowanne is his cousin. If the Ring isn't found, they will be the obvious choices for the throne, especially if they're married.'

'What does the Ring Fire tell you?' purred Fleabag unexpectedly.

'The Ring Fire? I've got a burning pain in my hands, if that's what you mean. I know I've got to do something, but I've no idea what. And I'm scared – even with a mighty cat like you by my side. Humans sort of need other humans too.'

Gemma thought for a moment. 'But I do think it's time we went north by northwest – with or without Rowanne. I'll talk to her.'

The cat twitched his whiskers. 'You're right, Rowanne was sent to be with us, but she has to make up her own mind to come. If she refuses, then you and I will set off together. When can you speak to her?'

'In about an hour when I dress her for dinner.'

'Good!' Fleabag said. 'Meanwhile, get packed. We leave in the morning. I've just got a few goodbyes to say.' And the grinning cat strode out of the room.

Gemma pulled out the clothes she had arrived in: trousers, shirt and leather jerkin. She held them up.

They didn't seem as big and baggy now.

She looked at herself in the mirror. She'd grown and filled out in the past weeks. Her cheeks were rounder and her freckles had become alarmingly brown and numerous. She straightened her blue dress. It was prettily made, with a white lace collar. The sort of thing she'd have treasured once, but it was already getting too small. Anyway, with winter approaching a dress would be of no use whatsoever.

She packed extra trousers and a woollen jacket. The walking shoes the queen had given her still fitted. She had no winter coat, so she pulled a thick blanket from her bed and rolled it up tightly. She'd need it at night and it'd be a cloak by day.

Gemma glanced at the clock. There was time to grab bread and cheese from the kitchen. She'd tell the cook she was on an errand for her mistress, then she might even be allowed cake.

At six o'clock she knocked on Rowanne's door.

When she went into Rowanne's room, she was relieved to see her mistress was alone, sitting at her dressing table in a cream satin underslip.

Curtseying, Gemma went to the wardrobe. 'What would you like to wear this evening, ma'am?'

Rowanne didn't look up from doing her nails. 'The turquoise blue. The jeweller has at last made a ring that is very like your drawing.'

She smiled at herself in the mirror. The look was unpleasant and triumphant. 'Tonight, Rupert and I will announce our engagement and I will wear the Ring of the Land.'

She held out her strong fingers and imagined the pale, fiery-hearted opal already there.

Gemma stumbled on the hem of the long evening dress. She did not know what to do with the anger in her chest, or the terrible burning in her hands. She covered up her clumsiness with a curtsey.

'Congratulations, ma'am!' she mumbled.

Rowanne swung round and glared at Gemma. 'You're not really pleased, are you?' she snapped.

Gemma clenched her fists. Her palms burned so fiercely that she almost expected to see them on fire.

Rowanne narrowed her blue eyes.

Gemma was frightened. But something had to be said. Now. The Fire Wielder was depending on her.

She laid the dress on the bed and opened her hands so the fire could burn if it wished.

'No, ma'am, I'm not happy. Just look at this dress, all frills and laces. You're not being true to yourself. You'll never be happy here!'

Rowanne shrugged and played with her hair. 'It's a means to a very useful end.'

The invisible heat burned Gemma's fingers. 'And *what* end is that? It's not the real Ring – neither will it be the real Fire. You'll have no joy from either of them. And just think, if you go through with this wedding you'll never have an adventure again.'

Gemma dumped the dress on Rowanne's bed. 'Get dressed properly and come north by northwest with me. Tonight!'

Rowanne's head went down. With flushed cheeks and flared nostrils she pulled her dagger from under a box of lace handkerchiefs. Then very quietly and dangerously, she pointed it at Gemma. 'Get out of my room. Immediately!'

Heart pounding, Gemma fled. As the door slammed behind her, a heavy thud hit the wood.

Fleabag was waiting in the corridor. 'Well,' he purred consolingly, 'she can't have wanted to kill you very much.'

'Why's that?' Gemma panted as she ran up the servants' stairs two at a time.

'Because,' puffed Fleabag as he flung himself into her room and landed on her bed, 'the Lady-Knight Rowanne de Montiland does not have a reputation for missing her mark.'

Gemma flung her uniform dress onto the bed, changed into her travelling clothes and grabbed her bundle. 'We're going – now.'

Fleabag ran, but Gemma hesitated.

'What's the matter?' he asked.

'It's just – well, I always longed for a room of my own more than anything. Now it's gone.'

'Forget it!' Fleabag urged as footsteps stomped up the servant's stairs.

'Is that a guard coming to arrest me?' Gemma gasped.

'*Run*!' Fleabag sprang down a dark passage and stopped by a stepladder that led to a skylight. 'Quick,' he gasped. 'Carry me.'

Moments later, Gemma was crawling out onto the roof. 'Oh help,' she panted, 'I feel dizzy. I don't like heights.'

Fleabag wriggling free from her arms. 'It's quite safe for humans. I've often seen men with hammers up here all day.'

'I'm not a man with a hammer,' whispered Gemma.

'Just follow my tail,' Fleabag instructed, leaping across the slates. Soon they came to an ivy-clad wall. 'This way,' Fleabag called out, springing lightly between the leaves. 'Throw your bundle down, first, then you'll have two hands.'

Gemma did as she was told, then followed,

squealing as the creeper branches shook and snapped under her weight.

Very soon, she joined Fleabag in the kitchen garden. Keeping low, they ran between the cabbages and rhubarb and out of the wicket gate at the back. Fleabag darted ahead to scout for soldiers. Then with a cheerful mew, he called her on.

Then, trying to look as they were only out for a stroll, they wandered through the backstreets of Rupert's city.

Gemma looked around nervously. It would be dark soon and the gates would close. She'd have been glad of a good sleep in her own bed before setting off. Facing a night alone – or almost alone – outside the city walls was not a cheerful prospect.

And how would they find north by northwest in the dark and without Rowanne to guide them?

But her thoughts were interrupted – by a heavy hand gripping her shoulder.

16 Autumn and Porridge

They entered a tiny, hot room, with a very old lady seated by an open fire, stirring a pot. She looked just like a witch.

'Bring her here, let me see her,' she cackled.

Gemma was pushed towards the light of the single candle, then she turned to glare at her captor.

He was a tall, dark-skinned young man from the South. His beard was not much more than fluff – and his eyes were smiling!

'Phelan!' Gemma gasped with delight, 'I'm so glad you're all right!'

'Who's this? Another waif and stray, or is it a spy?' the old woman croaked though empty gums.

'Auntie, this is the girl I told you about who saved my life,' Phelan explained.

'What's she doing here?'

'It's dark outside, she was frightened.'

The old woman snorted contemptuously.

'That's true,' Gemma admitted. 'But worst of all, I've lost my cat, he was in the street with me. I'd be a lot happier if he was here too.'

'If you mean this one,' Auntie prodded a black lump of fur with her toe, 'he found his own way in.'

Fleabag purred and rolled over to toast his back by the fire.

Gemma sank to the floor and hugged him. 'Yes, everything's all right now.'

'Is it really?' asked Phelan. 'You looked worried sick out the street.'

'I was,' she replied, then sitting on the hearthrug, she told the whole story.

Auntie scratched her hairy chin as she listened. 'Humf. Very well, you can spend the night by the fire, but I have some advice.'

Gemma looked up expectantly. The old lady gave her a rusty pair of scissors. 'Cut your hair. The prince's soldiers are looking for a girl. You've got a lad's clothes already, but your hair's too pretty and your voice is all wrong. You'll never pass as a boy. Shut your mouth and play stupid, then you might win through. The lad here will help you slip out of the city in the morning. He'll set you on the road.'

With that, the old crone slopped greasy stew into bowls. When they had all eaten, she climbed stiffly up the stairs to her bed.

When she had gone, Gemma whispered, 'I'm glad you found your Auntie. I thought you had no family?'

Phelan laughed out loud. 'This is a thieves' hide-out. She's sister, mother and aunt to us all! Now, try and get some sleep. Goodnight.' Then Phelan crept softly up the stairs, leaving Gemma and Fleabag alone by the fire.

Before dawn, Phelan reappeared and led Gemma silently through the dim streets to an unguarded part of the wall with a small door.

126

Phelan picked the lock with wire, then pointed out a road. 'That goes north, then there's a northwesterly turning on your left in a few miles that will lead to the university. The Ring might be hidden there – with the wise. Good luck.' He turned to go.

Gemma grabbed his coat. 'Won't you come with me?' she begged. 'Even with Fleabag, I can't pretend I'm not scared.'

Phelan shook his head. 'What have rogues and criminals to do with the Ring Fire? I'd put it out as soon as look at it!'

Gemma felt her palms tingle warmly. It wasn't an angry feeling like night before. 'I – I don't think you would put it out. In fact I think it likes you.'

But Phelan had already gone.

With a heavy heart, Gemma picked up her bundle and followed Fleabag onto the road.

The first few days passed pleasantly enough, until the food ran out. Fleabag caught a rabbit, but Gemma could not cook it as she had neither knife to clean it nor a tinder-box to make a fire. She quickly found that too many nuts and berries made her stomach ache, so she survived by scrubbing farmhouse floors and washing clothes in exchange for food and shelter.

They made good progress, but Gemma often had

the feeling she was being watched or followed.

The leaves slowly turned rich gold and then they fell. Autumn was coming to an end and the winds were blowing cold.

Gemma was worried. She was halfway though the year and a day allowed to find the Ring, but she was quite alone in a strange part of the land, with no idea whether they were even going in the right direction.

'I wish I had a clue whether I'm doing this right,' she sighed.

One chilly evening, Gemma had no work and no sheltering barn. Her blanket was damp and smelly from heavy rain and she felt ill. A shepherd's hut kept the wind off and Gemma and Fleabag snuggled up together in a corner. It was a long, miserable night.

At first light, Fleabag brought Gemma two harvest-fed rats, but his efforts were not appreciated.

Gemma peered over the blanket with feverish eyes. 'I need water, but you can't carry it. Oh, I feel so ill.' Then she pulled the blanket up over her head and fell back to sleep.

Fleabag climbed up a dry-stone wall to watch the road for passers-by. If Gemma didn't get help soon, she'd become very ill. She needed humans and cups of water and warm blankets. This was no time to worry about what life might be like in a circus.

He'd just have to talk his way out of that one, if it came to it.

One farmer's lad gave Gemma a drink, but no one seemed to want to take her home. As night began to fall and the freezing wind whipped the remaining autumn leaves into a frenzied dance, three dark shapes appeared on the road. It was a man on horseback leading two ponies. Something about the figure made him nervous. Should he run and hide, or stay and beg help?

He thought of Gemma shivering violently.

As the horses drew level, Fleabag plucked up all his courage, balanced, then took a flying leap onto the pommel of the rider's saddle.

The horse snorted and reared. The rider jumped, then a woman's voice swore roundly.

'Fleabag, you wretched animal. You'll be the death of me if I'm not the death of you first!'

Fleabag's fur bristled. 'Trust me to pick on *your* horse when I need real help. I'll go and find someone I can trust,' and he tried to jump down.

But Rowanne de Montiland had him firmly by the scruff of his neck. She reined in her horse and looked Fleabag in the eye. 'Don't judge me by what you think you know. Where's Gemma? What's the matter?'

The cat sagged in her hands. Even Rowanne's help

was better than none. 'Let me breathe and I'll show you,' he said.

She let him jump down and she sprang from the saddle after him. Within minutes, she had Gemma wrapped in dry blankets and astride the horse in front of her. Fleabag chose a pony laden with bundles, and snuggled into a small gap, then they set off again.

At the next farm, the farmer's wife regarded Gemma suspiciously. Autumn fever was a dreaded illness. But she changed her mind at the sight of gold.

For three days, Rowanne sat by Gemma's bed, feeding her sips of water and gruel. At night, Fleabag curled up by Gemma's feet, dozing lightly and opening an eye at the slightest sound.

On the fourth day, Gemma got up. She was still weak, but as she sat next to the fire wrapped in rugs and sipping soup, Rowanne told her what had happened since they had left Rupertsberg.

'The night you ran away, I told Rupert I had sweating sickness. I sat up all night and all the next day, just thinking. I was furious at first, of course, but then I realized that you were right. Rupert was unjust and greedy, oppressing his people and only interested in himself.

'The next day, I told Rupert I'd dreamed the Ring Fire spoke to me, telling me not to marry until I'd completed my quest, and that I had to set off straight away. He was livid and didn't want me to go. Then I told him I'd also dreamed of where the queen's Ring was hidden.

'"I need to find the *real* Ring," I said. "We'll look foolish if someone else gets it." He understood that. I said if no-one found it within the year and a day, then we'd stand a good chance of getting away with the one he'd had made.'

'All those lies!' Gemma winced.

'I don't like lying either, but it got me around Rupert. He's cunning, but not very clever. Eventually he agreed to providing me with travelling clothes, money and an escort of mounted soldiers, But when everything was ready, he insisted I waited so we could celebrate his birthday together.'

'Why did you agree?' Fleabag growled.

Rowanne shrugged. 'He'd kitted me out well, I had to be a bit nice to him in case he changed his mind.' Then Rowanne chuckled. 'But before I left I gave Rupert lots of promises and kisses, then I pushed the imitation ring onto his little finger so hard, I swear it'll never come off again!'

'So, what happened to the soldiers?' Gemma asked.

Rowanne's smile broadened. 'I didn't want them to know where we're heading, so I led the escort south, then after two days, I took them to an inn and got them drunk. When they were all asleep, I slipped away. I took the horse and ponies along a streambed so they wouldn't find my tracks. Then I came north, travelling only by night and leaving false trails here and there.'

Then she leaned over and rubbed Fleabag behind his ears. 'And it's good to see even you!'

Eyeing her knee-high boots, the cat permitted himself a small purr.

Next day, Gemma was well enough to travel and they set off. Rowanne gave her a plump little dappled pony called Porridge and Fleabag found a comfy perch on a pannier.

The land was a wide, open plain, and the wind whistled mercilessly across the emptiness. The few trees were now stripped quite bare and the days were very short. Ice formed on the horses' water pails and they chose an inn rather than a barn to sleep.

'I've been thinking,' said Rowanne one morning. 'It's only a short detour from the road to the university town of Porthwain. It is still very much north by northwest of Harflorum, so we aren't really going out of our way. What better place to hide the symbol of kingship than in the seat of wisdom? It must be there. We will ask at the university!'

'We could try,' Gemma agreed tentatively, remembering what Phelan and the ravens had said.

Fleabag wasn't so sure. 'So, how do we go about this?' he yawned as they settled down that night. 'Will you go up to one of the professors and say, "Anyone here got the queen's Ring? Can we have it? Thanks!"'

Gemma gave his ear a tweak. 'Don't get Rowanne's back up,' she whispered. 'We need her.'

Taking the easterly turning at the next crossroads, another day's ride brought them within sight of Porthwain. The 'walls' were scattered remnants of broken masonry, although a beautifully made wrought iron gate was hanging askew in one of the gaps.

Once inside the town, they found a sprawling collection of once-imposing buildings. They asked one or two passers-by for directions to an inn. One answered in the ancient – and incomprehensible – language of academics. Another leaned back against a wall and stroked his chin, then after a pause, began, 'Well, it depends what you mean by "inn". In the time of King Thributhious the Great, an "inn" implies a den of iniquitous living where brawls and gambling were to be expected. But in more recent times the usage has become changed to a house for business transactions to be worked out while the participants eat together late into the night. Now, if you want somewhere to gamble...'

Rowanne and Gemma looked at each other in horror. 'No, thank you, we just want somewhere to stay the night and rest our horses.'

'Ah!' the man's eye gleamed, 'you're taking the definition as proposed by Teumious in his erudite essay...'

But they never heard the rest. Gently they nudged their mounts onwards, leaving the man expounding to himself.

All the buildings were old and in a poor state of repair. Everywhere they looked, the people seemed preoccupied with nothing, or standing on street corners talking loudly. Most of the townsfolk seemed well fed and dressed, the place was suffering from neglect rather than poverty.

At last they turned a corner and saw an ancient, very low building with a black wooden door in a skewed frame. Over it hung the sign of a bush. An inn!

They knocked and a short, fat woman answered. She had flour up to her elbows and a friendly face. Here at last was someone who might be helpful.

'Do you have a room for two, please?'

'Yes, yes, come in,' smiled the woman.

Rowanne stepped over the threshold, but as Fleabag sprang out of his pannier to follow her inside, the woman's foot shot out. 'But no cats! Especially black ones. Bad luck, go away, shoo!' And she spat.

Fleabag narrowed his eyes and hissed back at her.

Rowanne's face fell with irritation. 'This is silly! Come on in Gemma, Fleabag's only a cat – he can sleep anywhere.'

Gemma shook her head, took Porridge's rein and turned away. 'We'll find somewhere else and call for you in the morning.'

Fleabag's fur stood on end. 'Rowanne's right, this is ridiculous!' he told Gemma. 'I'm very clean and I'm not bad luck!' With that he strode past the woman.

But she grabbed a broom. 'I said *scram*!' she yelled, whacking it down hard.

There was nothing for it.

They all ran.

17   An Invitation

Everywhere they went they got the same reaction. At the signs of the Bull's Head, the Two Lanterns and the Dancing Bear: no cats allowed, especially black ones.

At last, at the Bush of Broom, Fleabag rolled in ash to make himself grey, then slipped away to hide in the stable with the horses.

At dinner that night, Rowanne overheard three students talking about the search for the Ring. It sounded as if any questers who visited that particular inn were told tall tales and relieved of their purses.

'If they only knew the truth – if they only *knew!*' spluttered one of the lads gleefully.

'A fool and his money are soon parted,' quipped another and raucous laughter filled the taproom.

Rowanne bought a jug of honey ale and put it on the students' table. 'May I join you? She asked. 'I've been travelling for many months with my squire over there,' she jerked a thumb at Gemma. 'We've only heard wild rumours and tales about the Ring – you seem to know something about it.'

A narrow-eyed youth passed over his drinking pot. Rowanne filled it to the brim. He swallowed it in one gulp and wiped his mouth on his sleeve. 'More,' he demanded bluntly.

Rowanne ordered bread and cheese all round and re-filled his mug. Then, returning his stare, she sat astride the stool opposite him. 'Now,' she said. 'You were saying?'

The lad licked his lips and began. 'There are stories of great magic and evil deeds. Only the Chancellor of All Wizards really knows of course, but it's said that the queen was put into a magical trance by that evil sorcerer, the Fire Wielder, then he cut the Ring from her hand.'

The student leaned across the table and in a hoarse whisper, he added, 'Then, by terrible spells, which blackened the sky and froze the blood of bystanders, the Fire was wrenched from the Ring. Until the two are brought together again, the land is in great peril.'

The other boys sniggered, but Rowanne ignored them. Keeping her gaze full on the lad, she topped up his drink once more. 'Go on.'

Leaning forward, his eyes widened, 'It's said the Fire cannot last without the Ring – or without some creature willing to carry it. But who could do that and live?'

His companions nodded in agreement

The student continued, 'Here, at the university, we know that it's only his Holiness, the Chancellor of All Wizards, who keeps the Fire alive by spells...' He dropped his voice, 'which are too terrible to speak of!'

Rowanne glanced around to see if the other students were still laughing. There was no flicker of a smile between them. If anything, they looked afraid.

Gemma wriggled back into the shadows, keeping her hands tightly closed under the table lest the burning in her hands flared up. Her cheeks flushed with anger at the boy's lies, but she sat in rigid silence, hardly daring to breathe.

The boy looked hopefully into the depths of his ale pot, then at Rowanne.

Ignoring this, she lowered her brows and stared into his face. At last, slowly and deliberately, she said, 'I don't believe a word of it.'

The boy's companions gasped, exchanging glances.

Gemma bit her lip. There'd be trouble now.

The student raised one eyebrow. 'Oh? Then perhaps you ought to meet the Chancellor of All Wizards to see for yourself how ill he looks with the effort of holding our land together with his spells and his will. Then you'll understand how urgently he casts his gaze around to seek the whereabouts of the Ring.

Only when it's found will peace and justice be restored. Without it, the peppering of riots and unrest will soon become war. This must be resolved quickly.'

He glared at Rowanne under his pale lashes, then gripping his pot, he thumped it on the table.

Rowanne pushed it aside, watching the candles flicker yellow light across the boy's face.

Sensing things were getting dangerous, the others pulled back.

Silence.

'Very well,' Rowanne said at last, 'although I'm a mere knight who has no understanding of magic, I would very much like to meet his Holiness, the Chancellor of All Wizards. How can it be arranged?'

Without breaking his stare, the student tapped the jug with his tankard.

Rowanne nodded to the landlord. 'Fill it up.'

The informant drank slowly, then licked his lips. At last he asked, 'What's your name?'

Rowanne told him.

'Tomorrow night you will be invited to dine in the Great Hall of the university. Nine o'clock sharp. Be ready.' He drained his drink, picked up his cloak, then left with companions.

The door banged behind them, leaving a chilling silence.

'You're daft!' announced Fleabag, perched on the wooden rail at the foot of Gemma's bed.

'I don't need your advice, *thank* you!' Rowanne replied coldly. She frowned at the dressing table mirror and continued putting on eye make-up. After a few moments, she turned to Gemma. 'When you've finished washing those disgusting paw prints from the window-sill, you must do my hair.'

'Don't you ever say "please"?' complained the cat. 'She's not your servant, you know.'

Rowanne was about to say, 'Of course she is,' then remembered and mumbled 'please', under her breath.

'Why're you going to all this trouble?' Gemma asked, surprised at her own daring.

Rowanne tutted. 'You won't understand.'

Gemma picked up Rowanne's brush. 'You're all dressed up and you've ordered a carriage, yet it's obvious the man hasn't got the Ring. The boy was spinning you a tale to get free drink.'

Fleabag spread his whispers, 'Or more likely, to find out what *you* know.'

Rowanne mixed her eye-colours vigorously in their little pots. She was angry. 'I'm sure he knows *something*

– and I intend to find out what. It'll be easier to get him to talk if I dress like a courtier rather than a knight.'

'But he'll be suspicious about what a lady like you is doing here. Wasn't the intrigued traveller a better disguise?'

Rowanne winced as Gemma tugged at a stray loop of hair. 'I can hardly go to dinner dressed in my leather trousers and mail coat, can I? If I wear formal knightly gear, they'll know I'm in the Queen's Guard. Luckily I put a dress or two in my bag. Don't worry. I know what I'm doing.'

Just then, a maid knocked on the door. Fleabag shot under the bed and hid.

'Your carriage is here, ma'am.' The girl stopped and peered at the end of Fleabag's tail which poked out from under the counterpane. 'Forgive me, ma'am, but there's a ball of fluff on your floor. I'll get a brush immediately.'

'No, no,' said Gemma hurriedly. 'It's my furry slippers. They're rather old and disreputable, but I'm very fond of them.' With that, she kicked the whole of Fleabag's backside right under the bed.

'As you wish,' the girl replied, and left the room.

Gemma draped a lacy stole over Rowanne's shoulders. 'Please take care,' she said.

'Of course I will. Don't fuss!' Rowanne snapped, and then she left.

Once she was alone, Gemma went to the dresser and picked up the gold edged invitation that had arrived that morning. 'To the Lady-Knight at the Bush of Broom. His Holiness the Chancellor of All Wizards requests the pleasure of your company for dinner at the University Great Hall.'

'Perhaps Rowanne was right,' sighed Gemma. 'She would have looked out of place dressed in chain mail at a formal dinner. But I wish she hadn't gone. I've a bad feeling about this. What do you think, Fleabag?'

But there was no answer.

Gemma knelt down and peered under the bed. Was he sulking because she'd called him 'a disreputable old slipper'? There was nothing there except a trail of ash and a half eaten mouse. Really! He could have had his snack outside.

She picked the poor thing up by what was left of its tail and threw it out of the window.

While Rowanne was being helped into the carriage, Fleabag had also leaped aboard and lay crouched under the seat, hidden by her silk skirts.

It was dark by the time they arrived at the piazza outside the Great Hall. A university footman opened the carriage door.

Rowanne stepped out. 'I am the Lady-Knight Rowanne de Montiland. His Holiness the Chancellor of All Wizards is expecting me.'

'Of course, madam,' the man bowed and led her up sweeping marble steps to a magnificent pillared entrance. At the top, enormous carved oak doors stood wide, golden light streamed from sconces across the white stone. The footman led her along an echoing corridor flanked by statues of the university's great men and women.

At last he stopped. He swung open another massive set of doors and puffed out his chest. 'The Lady-Knight Rowanne de Montiland,' he announced pompously. As she stepped inside, the doors shut behind her with a dull thud.

Fleabag had kept out of sight, springing from statue to statue all the way up the corridor, but hadn't quite kept up. Now he was left hiding in the cobwebs behind the effigy of a cross-looking old woman. He said something very rude in rat language and washed himself thoroughly.

'Rowanne's mad,' he muttered. 'I can smell only trouble ahead. And what's worse, she's given her full name and title. Even kittens know that you never do that – especially to a *wizard* – it practically invites them to work spells on you.'

Once he had cleaned the tickly ash from his fur, Fleabag curled up for a catnap. To get that stupid woman out of this mess was going to need brainpower – and that required sleep.

His Holiness the Chancellor of all Wizards was tall, slim and elegant. He had neither the white whiskers nor the pointed hat that Rowanne had half expected. Like all the people from the West, he was fair and broad-boned, and his beard and hair were immaculately cut. He was dressed in a vermilion silk robe that was embroidered with gold and yellow flames all the way from the floor-sweeping hem to the superbly cut collar at his throat.

As Rowanne walked forward, the chancellor stood quite still in the centre of the circular room. The walls were plain white stone with windows set up high, meeting to make a glass-domed roof.

With a twist in the pit of her stomach, Rowanne realized that his clothes copied the formal garb of the true Fire Wielder – and the room was an imitation of the Hall of Light.

She curtseyed, as she felt it was expected.

The chancellor's face loosened into a smile. 'My dear,' he crooned. 'Welcome.' He stepped forward and stretched out his left hand towards her.

Rowanne's face contorted in horror and amazement. '*No*,' she gasped, meeting his ice-blue eyes.

For on his finger was a huge ring set with an opal.

… And the opal had no fire at its heart.

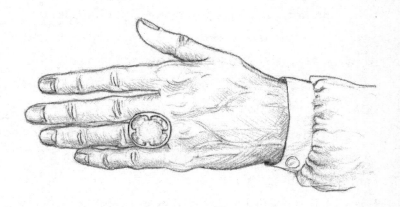

18   Dining on Spells

Ignoring her discomfort, the chancellor led Rowanne to a table laid with cut crystal glasses and exquisite bone china plates.

With perfect courtesy, he helped Rowanne to her seat. Another, smaller door opened and a tall, thin young man entered, dressed in a grey silk tunic and trousers. He bowed and kissed Rowanne's fingers. As he stood, she knew she recognized him, but could not think where they had met.

'Allow me to present my son, Sethan.'

Sensing Rowanne's hesitaton, the chancellor continued, 'It was he, of course, whom you met at the Bush of Broom last night. He was so impressed by your generous hospitality to a poor student that he begged to be allowed to return the honour tonight. He will be waiting on us.'

Rowanne tried to murmur something about it being a pleasure to buy the lad a drink, but a sweet-scented white wine was already being poured, and Sethan was organising servants with trays of delicacies.

The courses came constantly, dish after dish. Rowanne was coaxed to taste everything. Each accompanied by its own wine or cordial, which she was urged at least to sip.

Slowly, Rowanne became aware that she was unsure of the conversation. The chancellor seemed to be telling anecdotes about his time as a student and how hard it had been. He described his struggle against all opposition to prove himself worthy to become chancellor. He explained how various divinations had revealed that still greater things were within his grasp.

Rowanne's head was muzzy, but she understood that he had acquired the Ring – he did not say how – to help him achieve the ultimate greatness for which he had been born.

'You see, my dear,' he patted her hand as Sethan passed a silver dish of chocolate truffles for her to try, 'I am destined to be the next Fire Wielder. But unlike the others, with my mystical powers I will reign for ever.'

Rowanne screwed up her eyes. His face seemed to be swimming in and out of her sight. One second he was huge and lowering over her, the next, he was so far away he had almost disappeared.

I must excuse myself, she thought. *I have to get some*

air and clear my head. But her feet and arms would not obey. She could only listen.

'Very soon, my dear,' the chancellor went on, 'something wonderful is going to happen. As you know, in the past, a king or a queen needed a Fire Wielder to reign with him or her, but...'

Here his face floated across the ceiling until Rowanne had to crane her neck right back to see him.

Let me out! she sobbed inside her head.

'But I will be *both* – I shall be the perfect ruler. Complete in myself.' He pressed his fingertips together and smiled. 'Forever.'

Rowanne wanted to say, 'No!' but her lips had become thick and heavy.

With a slight nod from his father, Sethan lifted one more glass to Rowanne's lips. 'Try this,' he murmured, 'it's the finest wine in father's cellar.'

Her throat tightened and she tried to push it aside, but inside her head she was slipping away to somewhere dark and empty.

As soon as the glass was set to her lips, she drank as thirstily as if she'd just crossed the southern desert. Everything she could see or hear shrank until she was only aware of the chancellor slipping the opal ring from his finger and holding it before a candle so the flame seemed to flicker within the stone.

Rowanne began to shake, her eyes staring wildly.

The chancellor beckoned his son. 'She's ready. Help me carry her.'

They laid her on a chaise longue that had been placed nearby. Servants removed the dining table and the bed was dragged into the centre of the room.

The opal ring and the candle were put on a little stand so Rowanne could see it, with the bright flame glinting through it.

Drawing up a chair, the chancellor sat beside her. 'You will answer all my questions, Lady-Knight Rowanne de Montiland. You will answer, the truth completely and utterly.'

'I will,' she replied.

Deep inside, the last part of herself struggled and screamed. She was bound by magic and drugs; alone, trapped, and no sword within reach. Not that she could have used it.

'What are you doing here?' asked the chancellor.

'I am searching for the queen's Ring,' she replied.

The chancellor touched his opal. 'Is this it?'

'I do not know,' Rowanne replied dully.

'Who is with you?'

'A girl and a cat.'

At the sound of the word 'cat' two things happened. Firstly, Fleabag woke from his doze and realized it was time to take his favourite advice and do some eavesdropping, and secondly, the chancellor faltered and went pale.

'Where is the cat now?' he demanded.

'I don't know. He was at the Bush of Broom, but he goes his own way. He turns up when he feels like it.'

'What is the cat's name?'

'Fleabag.'

'Is that all?'

'Yes.'

Fleabag smiled in his whiskers, glad that no one alive knew his real name, so no spells could be put on him – as long as he didn't eat or drink in this place.

The chancellor spoke quietly to his son, 'As long as the cat isn't black, we've nothing to fear. The time of our downfall cannot be yet. The prophecy spoke of glory before the end.'

He turned back to Rowanne. 'Who is the girl? What is her name?'

'She is a guttersnipe, Gemma Streetchild. She travels with me and acts as my maid.'

'Of no importance, father,' said the boy. 'I saw her last night. She was a scared brat cowering in the corner and shaking at the sight of me. She cannot possibly be the Fire Maiden of whom we were warned.'

Again Fleabag sighed with relief. Gemma had never known her real name. 'Streetchild' was a nickname given to her at the palace.

'What do you know about the Ring?' the Chancellor persisted.

Mechanically Rowanne replied, 'The Fire Wielder took the Fire from the Ring. He holds the flame in the Hall of Light until the Ring is found.'

'And you are on the quest.'

'Yes.'

'Why did you come *here* to look for it?'

Fleabag held his breath. What would she say? Would she explain about the Ravens, or Gemma hearing the Ring Fire speak? So far, the Chancellor was asking all the wrong questions. As long as he kept off tack, all might yet be well.

Rowanne was speaking again. 'I came here because I reasoned that if the Ring is not kept in a palace, then it must be resting in the halls of wisdom.'

'Why did you come here tonight?'

Rowanne's voice dragged more and more slowly. 'Because the boy in the inn... made me suspect... that the chancellor might know something... to help me find the Ring.'

'By the Quenching of the Fire! She doesn't know!' The boy stamped in fury and frustration.

'I'm not so sure. I think the truth drug is fading.'
He held the final wine bottle up to the light. 'More
might kill her and I don't want that – not until I've
drained her of everything she knows.' He tapped his
teeth thoughtfully. 'I just haven't touched on the right
trigger question. What have I missed?'

The chancellor paced around the circular chamber,
stroking his beard. For several minutes the swish of
his silken robes was the only sound.

'Father,' said the boy at last. 'She has fallen asleep.'

The man strode back to Rowanne and lifted one of
her eyelids. He clicked his fingers a few times, but
there was no response. He sighed. 'We'll learn no
more tonight. It's frustrating for I believe we're very
close to the answer. I need to question her again.'

'In the morning?' Sethan asked.

'No, I must supervise the Convocation of the Wise,
but I may be able to slip away in the afternoon.'

Then he held up one hand. 'Even better, I will
cancel the dinner with the professors of philosophy in
the evening. They'll be so busy worrying about what
is meant by "dinner" they won't notice anyway. Make
sure she is comfortable during the day. She'll only
sleep I expect. At dusk I will say the spell that will
take her mind into my own.

'We'll arrange for her corpse to be found at the

bottom of a wall or something. Take her away and get some sleep boy. Tomorrow will be a long day.'

Fleabag soon found a way out of the Hall. Doors had been left open all over the place. Although the kitchen rubbish bin looked most tempting, he could not risk eating anything in case it was magic or drugged.

First he had to get back to Gemma to tell her what had happened. Because he'd travelled blindly beneath a carriage seat, he hadn't been able to see or smell the route, so it was almost dawn before he found the Bush of Broom once more.

All the doors were locked, and Gemma's window was fastened against the night's chilly wind. There was nothing to do except curl up in the stable. But even deep in the warm straw, he couldn't sleep. At dawn, he went out again.

Gemma did not sleep well either. She had expected Rowanne back late, but the morning light showed her bed had not been slept in. Gemma woke, stiff and muzzy, and went to the pump in the yard to fetch water. She never saw much point in waiting for a maid to do what she could manage perfectly well for herself.

Once again, she shivered with the strange notion that she was being watched. She hadn't felt it since before she had fallen ill in the shepherd's hut. She told herself not to be so silly, and splashed icy water on her face. She fed the horses and nudged Fleabag awake with a friendly toe under his black pelt.

But it didn't feel like Fleabag.

She looked closer. It was a human head, hidden under the straw. For a second, she hesitated. Should she call the innkeeper? Was it someone on the run or

just sleeping rough? Her hands tingled as she pushed the straw aside. The figure was lying very still, perhaps pretending to be asleep, or dead.

Grabbing a pitchfork, she lowered her voice and said, 'Stand up. I want to talk to you. Do as you're told and I won't hurt you.'

The young man clambered to his feet and smiled. 'Hello Gemma.'

'Phelan?' she lowered the pitchfork. 'What are you doing here skulking like a thief?'

He grinned, showing strong white teeth. 'I *am* a thief, in case you'd forgotten.'

At that second, Fleabag sprang into the stable, wet, cold, and in such a panic he made the horses start. Phelan turned and quietened them with a sure hand.

'Quick, quick,' howled the cat. 'Grab what you can! Get out of here. The whole town is after us!'

Gemma looked around nervously.

'I know which horses are yours,' Phelan said. 'I'll get them saddled. Get your things and meet me in the courtyard.'

'Quick, hide me, get me out of here!' Fleabag wailed.

Gemma had never seen the cat really ruffled before. 'I'll pack you in the luggage.'

Scooping him up, she wrapped him in her towel

and ran. Upstairs, Gemma flung clothes into bags while Fleabag stalked the room uneasily recounting the night's adventures. 'I got back here just before dawn, but couldn't sleep. I knew Phelan had been following us for some time, so I found him and told him we needed help to free Rowanne. I tried to get in to warn you, but the door was locked. You know this place has a thing about black cats?'

Gemma nodded as she pushed Rowanne's riding boots into the recesses of her bag.

'Well, there's some sort of prophecy that a Fire Maiden and a black cat will be the downfall of this chancellor. 'I couldn't resist it, could I? It was too good a joke to miss. I simply had to give them all a scare and have some fun. As soon as it was light, I went back and climbed the roof of the Great Hall. Right at the top, I paraded around with my tail in the air, declaring at the top of my voice the imminent demise of the chancellor and all his followers.

'You'd never believe the commotion I caused. I'd have kept my whiskers and tail to myself if I'd known. I soon had archers shooting at me, wizards chanting at me, and lawyers yelling legal clauses – though *my* "clawses" were better than theirs!

Gemma groaned at his pun. 'But what *happened*?'

'At first I just laughed, but then they set the dogs

on me, not just nice little lap doggies like the ones at the palace – you know, the sort you say "meow" to and they turn pale and run. No. These were *proper* dogs. With *teeth*.' Fleabag bared his fangs to demonstrate.

Then he stopped talking and cocked an ear. 'And I think I can hear them a few streets away. Is that Rowanne's perfume? Good, smother me in it so I don't smell of cat.'

Gemma picked up the bottle and puffed the spray liberally all over his fur. 'You look a mess,' she chided. 'What's this? Duckweed?'

Fleabag chuckled. 'I got away by jumping into a pond. The dogs lost the scent completely, then I crept round the outside of the city. Oh, I thought I'd never see you again!' and he jumped up and licked her chin.

'No time for being daft,' she laughed. 'Come here.' She dumped him on top of a load of dirty washing. 'I'll wrap you in this, but you have to stay still.' Then she pushed both cat and laundry into a saddlebag.

'Yuck!' Fleabag moaned from under the leather flap. 'Now I stink of human armpits.'

'Shut *up*!' she warned, shoving him deeper. 'Don't move a whisker.' She took coins from Rowanne's purse and left them on the table for payment, then swinging the bags over her shoulders, she staggered out into the courtyard.

Phelan was there with the horses bridled and saddled. He loaded up the panniers, then handed her a dollop of mud. 'Dirty yourself up – good, you look like a boy urchin now. Keep quiet, I'll do the talking.' He mounted Rowanne's horse lightly and trotted out into the street.

The sounds of dogs howling were now only a few streets away. They obviously had some sort of a trail, but was it leading this way?

Gemma hoped not.

19   Fire Maiden

Porthwain did not have a proper garrison. A few raggle-taggle soldiers kept a semblance of order, but they were not trained like the Queen's Guard.

A man dressed in the university's blue uniform, challenged the fugitives with a raised sword. Even Gemma could see he didn't know how to use it.

'Halt!' he demanded. 'Who goes there?'

'Slump forward and cough loudly,' Phelan whispered. 'And keep coughing.'

Phelan put on a thick Southern accent. 'Tis only a poor man from the South, Phelan Muckraker and his brother Gorthrod. We came to see the good doctors of this town, but they cannot cure him.'

Gemma coughed until she felt her lungs would burst.

Phelan leaned across the horse's neck and made sure he spat when he spoke. 'Tis sad, my brother seems to have the plague and…'

The man staggered back wiping the spit from his face. 'He's got the plague? Get *out*!' he screamed.

Gemma could not stop giggling. She buried her

head in her cloak, hoping her convulsive shaking would be taken for fever.

Passers-by yelled 'Plague!' and threw stones and dung.

Phelan grabbed the pony's reins and spurred his horse towards the open countryside. Galloping wildly, they fled past the massive dogs straining at their leashes, but the cry of 'plague' had gone before and the dogs were checked.

In the depth of his saddlebag, Fleabag chuckled as he heard the dogs howling to their humans that there was a cat with the horses. But the masters were either too stupid to understand the dog-speech, or too frightened of the plague to do anything.

Within minutes, Phelan, Gemma and Fleabag were riding down the hill and away from the town. After an hour they came to a wood where they drew rein and stopped to rest the horses. They had a few minor cuts between them, but none of them was badly hurt.

Fleabag climbed out of his prison and rolled on the grass to rid himself of the stink of perfume and dirty clothes. 'Clever Phelan,' he purred. 'That was almost worthy of a cat's wit!'

Phelan grinned and bowed. 'Sir Cat, I am honoured.'

Gemma helped him unsaddle the mare. 'What are

you doing here, Phelan? I am so pleased to see you, but where did you spring from? And how did you know which horses were ours?'

Phelan lifted the panniers from the pony's back. 'I was worried when you left Rupertsberg. I wanted to go with you, but I'm only a common thief and you're on the queen's business.

Gemma shook her head. 'I still need friends.'

'You've seen the Ring Fire,' Phelan added with awe. 'I shouldn't be anywhere near you.'

'But…' Gemma began.

Fleabag raised a paw. 'Let him finish. 'We'll talk about things being right and wrong later.'

Phelan nodded. 'Well, I followed you, although I lost you for a while. I guessed you'd be heading for Porthwain as it's the nearest town, and I had some luck with a lift on a cart. I waited outside the town walls, but you didn't come. I thought I'd gone the wrong way until I saw you arriving two days ago. I met up with old Fleabag in the market yesterday and he told me everything you've been up to. He said he had a feeling you might need me, so I hid in the stable – then you trod on me.'

'We're both glad you were there,' Gemma stroked Fleabag. 'I couldn't bear to think of my friend as dog-meat.'

Fleabag shivered. 'Don't say such things please, even in jest!'

Gemma shrugged. 'Sorry. Anyway, now I know why I thought someone was watching me.' She tugged Fleabag's tail gently. 'I wish you'd told me who it was, you wretched animal. I've been quite scared at times.'

'You never asked.' Fleabag replied, chewing a passing flea.

Gemma scratched behind his ear. 'I forgive you – this time,' she added. 'But now we're safe, you must tell Phelan what happened to Rowanne.'

Fleabag stopped washing and for once, cracked no jokes. When he finished his story, Gemma shook her head. 'I've no idea how we're going to rescue her. Facing danger is one thing, but we'd need the Fire Wielder himself to stand up to the chancellor.'

'Do we *have* to rescue her?' Fleabag muttered, rolling onto his back so the wintry sun could warm his tummy.

'Of *course* we do!' Gemma replied indignantly. 'She may be a cat-hater, but she was sent on this quest too – by the Fire Wielder.' She paused. 'If the Chancellor of All Wizards says the spell to take Rowanne's mind from her, then he'll know everything she knows. He'll follow us and maybe we'll lead him to the Ring. We must rescue her to protect the quest.'

'True,' mused the cat in his upside-downy voice, as he picked at another wandering flea. 'But wouldn't everything be easier without her?'

'No!' Gemma replied firmly. 'Bother it, we need her!'

Fleabag wriggled hard, rubbing his back on the rough ground. He had a look of intense concentration on his whiskers. At last he sat up. 'Oh, very well. We'll rescue her, but I beg you, never tell any of my relatives what I'm about to do, or I'll be called a poodle for the rest of my days.'

'That's a relief,' Gemma said mischievously. 'If Rowanne wasn't with us you'd have to annoy me instead. I don't think I could face that.'

'Mind you,' Fleabag added, 'if she threatens me one more time after this, I'm off. You can come with me if you like, but a cat can only take so much. Now, let me get some sleep so I can think.' Then he jumped into a saddlebag for a snooze.

No one spoke for a while. The clouds grew thick and heavy, making the afternoon almost dark. Phelan set a trap for any passing game, then moved the horses and baggage to a small hollow where he lit a fire and roasted a squirrel. While it cooked, Gemma and Phelan huddled in blankets listening to the wind rattling the bare branches of the trees.

'Why did you run away at the hostel?' Gemma asked at last. 'You didn't even say goodbye.'

Phelan shrugged. 'My friends and I tried to kill you. I was the cause of your arguing with the Lady Rowanne and not sleeping in luxury in the palace. I'd done you nothing but harm. Anyway, being caught in my company is no great honour. If I'd been recognized and put in prison, they might have taken you as well. As I told you before, Prince Rupert has no great reputation for justice.'

'I was lonely when you went. Oh, I know I've got Fleabag, but he's not always there and I need as many friends as I can get.'

'Even Rowanne?'

'She may be a pain, but we were told to help each other. She has been good to me in an odd sort of a way. I can't just let her die. That's not the right way to do things, is it? It's just like we couldn't let you die. For the moment at least, we belong together.'

Phelan pulled his blankets closer. The day was getting colder and he could sense the night would be worse. 'For what it's worth, I'll help. Now look, I don't know what sort of idea that fur-brained cat of yours comes up with, but we'd better know what we're going to do if – I mean *when* we help her escape. We'll

165

probably be fleeing in the dark and I smell snow in the air. We'll need to have somewhere we can run straight to and rest, especially if anyone gets injured.'

Gemma climbed to the lip of the hollow and surveyed the countryside beyond the wood. 'There are farmhouses with barns and sheds further along the road. But any pursuers will search them first. A lot depends on how fit Rowanne is. If she can ride, we'll make it, but if there's a hue and cry or if she's still unconscious, we'll need somewhere closer to hand. Here's as good a place as any, I suppose,' she added, shivering.

'Safe, but cold,' Phelan added.

'I'm freezing already,' Fleabag mewed as he jumped out of his saddlebag. He yawned and stretched his back, tail and all three paws. 'And what's more,' he added, 'I can smell perfectly good squirrel burning.'

'Now,' said Fleabag, his mouth full of meat, 'as I told you this morning, there seems to be some sort of prophecy about a Fire Maiden and a black cat which terrifies the wits out of this chancellor. I pushed my luck a bit this morning, by acting the black cat part, but what I really needed was a Fire Maiden with me. So what we will do is this...'

Phelan left the horses in a small side-alley near the Great Hall. He'd taught them to come when he whistled.

As there were few guards of any sort, they managed to reach the main door before they were challenged.

Dressed in Rowanne's clothes, Gemma held herself tall and straight. When a footman answered the door, she lowered her voice and tried to sound confident, 'I have had a dream. I need to speak to the Chancellor of All Wizards immediately.'

The man looked down his nose at Gemma. 'And may I ask the nature of this information, madam?'

Gemma swallowed hard. 'There is great danger at the threshold of his house.'

The guard paled, but led the Gemma and Phelan to the doors of the imitation Hall of Light.

'You may leave us!' Gemma waved her hand imperiously at the man.

He looked surprised but obeyed. As soon as he was out of sight, Gemma threw back her cloak to show the flame-red dress she had borrowed from Rowanne.

Phelan lit the two large torches he had smuggled in under his cloak. He handed them to Gemma, and smiled. 'You look just the part.'

It was getting dark and the firelight danced on the great oak doors as Phelan knocked.

There was no answer, but low voices could be heard within.

With a pounding heart, Phelan threw the doors open and announced, 'The Fire Maiden has come with her black cat to claim your life. Tremble and fear!'

In the middle of the hall, the Chancellor of All Wizards and his son were studying a heavy illuminated manuscript.

Both men looked up. Sethan went pale, but the chancellor threw back his head and laughed. 'Don't be silly,' he snapped. 'Go and play your games somewhere else.'

But Gemma did not move. 'This is no game,' she held the flickering lights high. 'The Ring Fire has come.'

While Gemma was talking, Phelan crept towards a figure on a couch in the far shadows of the room.

Gemma watched him carefully.

He nodded once. It was Rowanne.

Now all they had to do was to get her out and run. Fear tightened Gemma's chest and blood pounded in her ears.

Phelan opened the satchel on his shoulder and let

Fleabag jump out.

In two bounds the cat had crossed the room and leaped onto the table, skidding to a halt on the book, sending an array of glass bottles and herbs crashing to the floor.

At the sight of Fleabag, the chancellor stopped laughing. He grabbed a stone pestle, threw – and missed.

Sethan sprang forward and grabbed Fleabag.

He twisted in the boy's grasp, scratching his face and eyes until blood flowed. Howling in agony, Sethan dropped the cat.

Fleabag sprang back to the table and faced his foes, ears flat, spitting and hissing.

'Father, help!' Sethan squealed.

Ignoring him, the chancellor took some chalk and drew magical signs on the floor, all the while chanting an ugly sounding rhyme.

'How… how did you get in here?' sobbed Sethan, nursing his face.

'The footman opened the door, stupid,' replied the cat. 'You should have had guards.'

Sethan stared wide-eyed. 'The cat… it *talks*!'

The chancellor rolled his eyes. 'Don't listen. It's a trick, a distraction.'

Sethan gulped. 'But how did they get in? The place

is ringed with magic. Only the Ring Fire itself could get past our spells.'

'Shut up!' yelled his father. 'A charm must have slipped somewhere. Probably one *you* made. I'm always telling you to be more careful. It *must* be your fault. The Ring Fire could not come this far north without me knowing. The Fire Wielder's every step is watched and reported to me daily. At this very moment he is asleep in the palace at Harflorum.'

The chancellor stood in the middle of his symbols, lifted his arms high and began a new chant. A wall of bright blue flames sprang up around him, then with a thunderclap, he flung a blaze of green at Gemma.

She thought of the Ring Fire. 'I won't forget,' she whispered. Gripping her torches with trembling hands, she lifted them higher.

The emerald flare fizzled.

More thunder – and the chancellor threw a purple flash.

Gemma screwed up her eyes and thought of the Hall of Light.

The purple faded too.

Drawing on all his strength, the Chancellor of All Wizards screamed, 'Bring me *power*!'

Sizzling lightning seared across the room.

Dropping her torches, Gemma grabbed the spell

book and pulled it over her head.

The lightning forked, flashed and hit the book.

'Not my precious spells!' The chancellor leapt through the blue flames to grab it back. The trailing skirts of his robe caught fire and he fell to the floor, screaming.

Sethan rushed to his side, but the hungry pool of cerulean engulfed him too.

Gemma could not bear their agony. She hadn't meant to hurt anyone. She reached out to help them, but both father and son cowered back at the sight of her. 'Not the Ring Fire! Take it away. It's burning us!'

The chamber was rapidly filling with attendants carrying water and fire brooms. No one could get near the raging blue flames – higher and higher they towered, licking the glass lantern roof.

Gemma cowered under the table as glass shattered and fell like deadly rain. A foot kicked at her legs.

It was Phelan dragging Rowanne. 'Too heavy… Help me. Got to run!'

Gemma tugged one of Rowanne's arms around her neck and between them they hauled her out of the room and along the corridor.

In the smoke and confusion, no one noticed three people and a cat running out of the front door.

20 Cottage in the Rocks

Everything was in turmoil when they reached the flight of stairs down from the Great Hall to the piazza below. Snow was falling, making the steps slippery. Hundreds of people were pushing and shoving – some trying to get inside with pails of water, others fleeing the burning building in panic.

The four were buffeted and shoved. Gemma and Phelan dragged the unconscious Rowanne between them, while Fleabag clawed the ankles of anyone in the way.

Phelan whistled, summoning the waiting horses, but the hubbub drowned him out.

The roar of flames behind them was coming closer.

'Wait here,' Fleabag yowled, then he darted between the thundering feet, risking life and paw to reach the little alley where the horses waited quietly.

With one leap, he gained the mare's saddle. Try as he might, he could not whistle. 'Come on, you silly animals, this is urgent!' he cajoled. 'If you don't move, your owners will be dead and there'll be no more oats!' He reinforced his point by applying a claw or two on the animal's withers.

The mare snorted and led the ponies gingerly through the flames, smoke and falling masonry until they reached the steps where Phelan and Gemma cowered with Rowanne.

A passer-by helped to heave the knight onto the back of her horse. 'There now, she'll be all right, I reckon, he said kindly. Then he caught sight of Fleabag seated grimly with Gemma on the pony. The gold of the flames reflected in their wide eyes.

The man shook his head. 'So it is true, the black cat and the Fire Maiden have come at last. All speed to you!'

Phelan nodded. 'Thank you.' Then he took the horse's rein and eased them through the crowds. Once they were clear of the tumble-down walls, they left the noise and turmoil behind and headed for the north road.

Fleabag jumped down and led the way to the little hollow where they had camped. Phelan threw blankets over the animals and coaxed the banked fire back into life. At last the three of them lay close together, trying to sleep, but it was a long, cold night.

At first light they struck camp. Rowanne was still in her strange slumber and did not stir. The snow had only left a light sprinkling, but the sky was lowering with promises of more.

Gemma chewed her lip. 'It's going to get worse,' she said, then turned to Phelan. 'Before we go, I need to get something straight. You've got to believe me when I say we need you. You aren't a bad person; in fact you're a very good friend. Please don't disappear again. I need help to get to – wherever I'm supposed to be going – and I can't look after Rowanne on my own. What's more, Fleabag needs someone to insult. Say you'll stay with us, *please*?'

Phelan kicked at the snow with the worn toes of his boots. He was quiet for a few moments. 'Very well, just until the lady is well enough to look after you all, and to make sure she's not going to desert you again.' He looked at Gemma squarely. 'I'll not stand for that a second time. But I'll keep out of the search for the Ring if you don't mind.'

Gemma nodded. 'I don't understand but thank you.'

Phelan helped Gemma heave Rowanne over the back of Pudding, the fat little pack pony, then he mounted the mare and took Pudding's rein. Gemma was glad to be back with Porridge again. Fleabag chose to walk.

'First, we must get back on the main road north by northwest,' Gemma said. 'I should've realized we were wrong when Rowanne said Porthwain was "slightly" out of the way.'

They rode with the watery sun at their backs for several days. The winds became increasingly bitter, then laden with icy sleet. Slowly the ground rose ahead of them into the foothills of the Gwithennick Mountains that stretched from east to west, as far as the eye could see.

One miserable morning they were camping in a barn – which was about as waterproof as a net curtain. Gemma was trying to make Rowanne drink a little, when Fleabag came and sat in front of the pile of spitting, damp sticks that passed for a fire.

'It's no good. I hate having wet fur. We have to find somewhere warm and stop for the winter.'

Phelan was sorting wood, looking for something dry enough to burn. He knocked a thick icicle off a branch. 'I'm with Fleabag,' he said. 'We need to stop to get Rowanne better if nothing else, and with all due respect, Gemma, I think you need time to think about what you're doing. Hearing voices that tell you to go north by northwest sounds a bit potty, if you don't mind my saying so. It doesn't mean it's not true, but you need a practical plan as well. Rest, warmth and food will help.'

Phelan stamped on a dead stick, snapping it loudly.

Gemma jumped, but Rowanne didn't flicker an eyelid. She was not improving.

'What month is it?' Gemma asked.

'November,' Phelan replied. 'Almost December.'

Gemma shook her head. 'We must keep going. The Fire Wielder told me he could hold the Flame for a year and a day – we've wasted too much time already. Perhaps we could find someone to take Rowanne in?'

'Where? The nearest town is Porthwain…' Phelan pointed up at the mountains. 'That's north by northwest. Snow will block all the roads soon – we won't be able to go forward or back. Like it or not, we're stuck. Let's just accept it and rest.'

Gemma sighed. 'I agree, but how shall we survive?'

Stepping outside, Phelan shielded his eyes from the biting winds and surveyed the terrain. 'What do you fancy? A farm where we can work for the winter and earn our keep, or a place of our own?'

Gemma bit her lip. 'The farms around here are very poor and rundown. They couldn't support us, however hard we work. We need our own place.'

Phelan nodded and stacked the firewood in a heap. 'You're right. Will you lend me the horse for the day? I'll ride ahead and see what I can find.'

'Good idea,' Gemma replied, handing him some

bread and cheese. 'Try and be back by nightfall, or we'll worry.'

Phelan wrapped himself in a blanket and saddled the mare. Outside, he hesitated and shivered. Where should he start? Everywhere looked so grey and miserable. The trees were like skeletons and the sky seemed to be perpetually weeping. Squeezing the horse's flanks with his heels, Phelan rode up the hill to the lane, then urging the mare into a trot, he set off.

'You know what Rowanne would say, don't you?' asked Fleabag unhappily.

'What?'

'"You'll never see that horse or that boy again. He'll ride away, sell it and go his own way." '

'Do you believe that?'

'No. Do you?'

Gemma shook her head. 'No. I always get a fierce burning feeling in my hands when something's wrong. I don't get that with him.' She poked at the fire, but the charred twigs fell apart and the flames went out.

'I wish you could make a real blaze with your burning hands,' moaned Fleabag.

'That would be nice,' Gemma sighed.

The hours dragged on in their grey, damp, unhappy way. In the early afternoon Gemma took the ponies for a run to warm them up a bit. As she returned, she could just make out a rider in the distance, coming down the road very fast.

She led the ponies inside and hid with bated breath behind the door as the heavy thud of hooves approached and slowed.

'What's wrong?' mewed Fleabag.

'It might be a wizard from Porthwain,' she whispered.

'He's coming from the north, silly,' Fleabag replied, slipping outside. He was back immediately. 'It's all right, it's Phelan.'

Gemma ran outside and waved as Phelan dismounted and lead his horse down the little slope to the derelict barn.

'I've found just the place!' he proclaimed breathlessly. 'It's a bit tumbledown, but it'll be perfect with a little work. It's a deserted goatherd's hut built into a small cleft. If we hurry, we'll just get there by nightfall!'

Unsaddling, he rubbed the mare down and let her graze. Then he helped the others pack. Gemma and Phelan heaved Rowanne across Pudding's saddle and tied her in place with a blanket.

The weather held dry, but a biting wind cut across the barren landscape as if it were driving them back from the foothills. As they went on, sharp rises of rocky outcrops dipped into marshy flats, then rose steeply again. But the road was fairly good and kept north by northwest, much to Gemma's relief.

A few crofters' cottages were dotted across the landscape. Skinny, chilled-looking cattle and sheep huddled in the lee of anything which afforded shelter.

As the light began to fail, Gemma became increasingly worried. The road was rising well above the plain and the rocks were slippery with evening ice. There were no buildings at all within sight.

Seeing the despair on Gemma's face, Phelan gave her a hearty slap on the back. 'Not far, look!' He pointed ahead to where the road detoured around a rockfall. There was still no sign of a dwelling of any kind.

Gemma bent her head doggedly to go on. 'I bet we've missed the cottage in the dark,' she complained to Porridge, patting his neck.

Just then, Phelan gave a whoop and sprang to the ground. He led the mare away from the road and across a short grassy slope towards a cliff... and then he disappeared.

'Phelan?' Gemma called out. 'Where are you?'

'Here!' his echoey voice replied. 'Come on!'

'Where? It's so dark, I can't see you.'

'This way.' Fleabag jumped down from where he'd been curled on Rowanne's back to help keep her warm. Pudding followed the cat and Gemma came next, leading the patient Porridge.

The cottage was little more than a roof across a wide split in a rock and the front was a stretch of dry-stone walling with a wooden door. But as Phelan had promised, it was better shelter than the old barn.

The cottage was roughly triangular, with two rooms. The door at the front was still more or less on its hinges, it had little roof left, but would shelter the horses from the wind. Behind this was a narrower chamber, deep inside the crevice. It was very dark and musty, but big enough to let everyone lie down comfortably.

Phelan managed to get a small fire going. Bread and water were passed round and, for the first time in over a week, everyone was warm.

Soon Phelan and Fleabag were asleep, but Gemma's night was disturbed by dreams. They seemed to be echoes of the things she used to see when she watched the Fire in the queen's Ring. As she dreamed, her hands burned more fiercely than ever.

She woke shivering, so she built up the fire and sat staring into the flames until dawn.

'What use are dreams?' Gemma asked herself. 'Phelan's right, me wandering off across the land is daft. What's a street urchin doing on this quest? Perhaps I only *wished* the queen sent me? What possible use could I be in affairs of state? What do I know about the Ring or the Fire?'

As dawn crept into the corners of the little shelter, Phelan rolled over and touched Gemma's hand. 'You were thinking aloud,' he said quietly.

Gemma hung her head. 'Sorry.'

'Don't be,' Phelan replied kindly. 'I… I didn't mean to make you doubt anything. I just thought you needed time to rest and think – to be certain of your direction. With winter coming on, it seemed like a good idea.'

Gemma blinked back tears. 'But I don't *know* what I'm doing or where I'm going, or even why. I don't know how anyone could ever hope to find the Ring – and how can I possibly be there when it happens? Rowanne might have some ideas, but she's in this strange magic sleep. I'm worried sick we came too late and that the spell to take her mind from her has already been said. Are we just carrying Rowanne's shell? Can we do anything?'

Phelan knelt by the knight. She was pale and her breathing was slow and shallow. He lifted her wrist and felt the throb of life in her veins.

'I don't know,' he said. 'I picked up some knowledge of herbs and fungi while living in the woods. I can try and rouse her. But in the end, I'd guess it'll need something stronger than potions to heal her.'

'More magic?'

Phelan shook his head. 'No. Something stronger even than magic.'

He left Gemma looking wide-eyed and worried as he got up to fetch water. He found Fleabag chewing a rather scrawny rat outside the door.

'Awful hunting around here,' he moaned. 'Couldn't you do better than this? I ordered the best hotel with room service and milk on a saucer every morning,' he grumbled, 'I'm complaining to the management!'

Phelan picked up the cat by his scruff and glared at him. 'I bested you in a fair fight once, cat, and I can do it again.' He gave Fleabag a friendly cuff as he put him down gently. 'So watch it!'

Fleabag looked as sheepish as a cat can. 'Would you care for some rat's leg – or maybe a nice bit of ear? A bit chewy but very tasty – *sir*?'

21 Fungus Soup

For the first few days, they divided their time between repairing the cottage and foraging for food. Fleabag caught some partridges and a hare and Phelan bought vegetables and hay from one of the nearby crofts.

Much of the roof-support timber was still usable. Phelan pushed the rafters back into place and Gemma helped him remake the roof with flat fir branches covered with turf. These they lashed down with ropes twisted from heather stems and weighted with small boulders.

There was plenty of dead wood for the fire and the cottage soon became warm and cosy.

Everyone began to feel better – except Rowanne.

One day Phelan came back with a large piece of bark and a bag of toadstools. Banking up the fire so it smouldered rather than burned, he scraped some greenish-grey slime from the bark into the cooking pot. This he mixed with water and let simmer for several hours. He would not let Gemma cook the evening meal, as the fire had to be kept at a steady

temperature and there was only one cooking pot.

Fleabag was not too bothered as he'd caught a trout in the stream and was quite happy to chew it raw.

Gemma made do with dried fruit and scowled at Phelan. 'What are you doing? I'm famished and that stuff stinks. I wouldn't eat it if I were dying of hunger.'

Phelan went on stirring the pot. 'You're not *supposed* to eat it. It's a potion. I'm using a powerful lichen which stimulates the mind. Its effects are dramatic. I've heard people jump over cliffs after drinking the juices, yelling a dragon is after them, although in reality it's just a mouse in the corner. The drink makes everything bigger and louder and brighter. I thought a few drops might do something for Rowanne.'

'Shock her out of it, you mean?'

'Worth a try?'

'Well, can you make her a nice person while you're at it?' enquired Fleabag. 'Turn her into a cat-lover so she can treat me with the respect I deserve.'

'She already *does* treat you as you deserve,' observed Gemma. 'Can you eat that fish in the other room with the horses or, even better, outside altogether? I can't stand the sound of you slurping when I'm so hungry.'

With a 'humph' of disgust, Fleabag picked up the remains of his meal and stalked out, tail erect and fur fluffed. The reception he got from the horses was similar and he ended up behind the woodpile in disgrace.

Crouched by the fire, Gemma was worried. 'What happens if Rowanne drinks it and tries to do something daft? We can't stop her, she's very strong.'

'I don't really know,' Phelan replied thoughtfully, 'but she's hardly moved or eaten for almost a month, so she'll be very weak. I reckon we can hold her down if she goes wild.'

Gemma still wasn't happy. 'How long will it take for the effects to wear off?'

'Usually about a day, but you can get flashbacks for up to a year.'

'Is it worth the risk? Is there something a bit less drastic in your bag?'

Phelan spread out the pile of toadstools. 'It's very difficult to find anything once the snow falls. I gathered these from a small wood in a hollow over the ridge. It's sheltered from the mountain wind and it's a lot milder.' He picked up a white puffball that looked soft and delicate. 'This one is called "Dreamcloud". It's a sleep inducer. And this,' he held up a thick liver-like fungus about the size of his hand, 'is delicious if fried, especially with fish. These orange ones I can dry and we can eat them at a pinch. They aren't poisonous, but they're very chewy and taste like old socks. It depends how hungry we get.'

'Oh look, on the floor, you found a mushroom.'

Phelan's thin hands grabbed the small brown fungus that he'd tried to keep out of sight. 'Don't – that's deathcap.'

'What's it for?' Gemma asked.

'There's enough poison in that to kill half of prince Rupert's army and make the other half very sick.'

'Ugh!' she jumped back. 'Why did you pick it?'

Phelan put it into his pocket. 'I don't know really.' Then he returned to stirring the pot.

At last the lichen was reduced to a greyish sludge in the bottom of the pot. He put two drops of the liquor into a cup of water and stirred it. 'Feed her this. If she starts coming to, then stop straight away. I don't want her going crazy.'

Gemma took the cup and picked up a spoon.

Suddenly she had such a stabbing pain in her hands that she dropped everything.

'Hey, watch out!' moaned Phelan. 'I had to climb a difficult tree to get that, then it took me hours to get the mixture right. Don't go flinging it around!'

'I couldn't help it,' Gemma squealed, clutching her hand.

'What's the matter?' enquired Fleabag, sliding around the doorpost. 'Pooh! what's that stink?'

'That "stink",' Phelan said, huffily, 'was the potion I've just spent hours brewing to try to revive Rowanne. Now Gemma's just flung half of it away.'

Gemma shook her head. 'I'm sorry. I got this stabbing pain.'

'Let's have a look.' Fleabag climbed into Gemma's lap. He sniffed and licked her fingers but there was nothing wrong.

'Never mind,' said Phelan. 'I have more. Just be careful this time, will you? Pass the cup.'

Fleabag put a paw on Gemma's arm. 'Wait. When Phelan passes you the mixture, just hold the cup for a minute and see what happens.'

Gemma looked at the cat. 'You're odd,' she said.

'Not as odd as I suspect *you* are,' he retorted. 'Now,

just do as you're told.'

Phelan mixed the potion again and passed Gemma the cup. Nothing happened.

'Now, bring the cup slowly towards Rowanne...'

'Ouch!' Gemma jerked her arms back, again spilling everything. 'I feel like I'm being burned!'

Fleabag sniffed at her hands again. 'I know what it is,' he announced triumphantly. 'It's the Ring Fire. The little bit of Fire you carry is warning you not to give that stuff to Rowanne. It's wrong for her.'

Gemma looked wide-eyed at the cat.

Then Phelan looked even more wide-eyed at Gemma. 'You mean you have the Ring Fire, and I've been treating you just like – just like *anyone!* I... I've even been rude to you... I'm sorry, I'm so sorry!' And before Gemma knew it, he was on his knees.

'Oh, don't be stupid!' Gemma snapped. 'I *am* "just anyone". If a street child can't be friends with a thief, what good is anything? You're my only friend apart from this disgusting cat who keeps trying to make me eat rat.'

'It was a very *fresh* rat,' muttered Fleabag.

'And what good are friends on their knees? I *need* people who are rude to me. Get up and insult me again, for goodness' sake! You're scaring me.'

Fleabag rubbed his nose under her chin and

purred. 'What're you getting upset about? You often get a burning in your palms when something's wrong, so why shouldn't the Ring Fire warn you not to give Rowanne the potion?'

'Because the Ring Fire is back at the palace with the Fire Wielder.'

'Except for the little bit he told you never to forget.'

Gemma opened her cupped hands and looked. They were just hands, stained and callused from hard work. Very ordinary hands indeed, except in the center of each palm, there burned a tiny speck of flame.

22   Ring Fire!

As everyone stared, Gemma's hands trembled and the light faded.

'Hold it steady!' Fleabag purred. 'Think of the Fire Wielder... Think of the queen...!'

Tears glistened on Gemma's cheeks. 'I'm scared,' she whispered. 'Help me!'

'The Ring Fire only stays where it is welcome,' said Fleabag quietly. 'Do you want to hold it?'

'Yes,' she replied. 'It's so beautiful and calm. I want it, but I'm scared as well.'

Phelan and Fleabag held their breath as the little

flame grew between Gemma's fingers.

'Look,' whispered Fleabag, 'Rowanne's eyelids are fluttering; she's looking at it. Take it closer, Gemma.'

Rowanne opened her mouth as if she was trying to say something, but couldn't.

'There,' said Gemma. 'Would you like to hold it?' She placed the flame within Rowanne's hand, but it slid like mercury back into Gemma's palm.

And where the flame had touched her, Rowanne began to move.

'Look at that!' gasped Phelan. 'Do it again!'

Gemma tried Rowanne's other hand. The same thing happened.

Rowanne's eyes opened wide with longing.

Fleabag said very softly, 'The chancellor tried to take her mind – try putting the flame on her head?'

The room was heavy with silence.

Gemma held her breath as she lifted the Fire towards Rowanne's face. 'Wake up,' she coaxed.

Rowanne stirred and tried to sit.

'As I said,' murmured Phelan, 'she needed something greater than magic.'

23 King of the Castle

Over the next few days Rowanne quickly regained her strength. 'I knew what was happening all time,' she explained. 'I just wasn't able to move or speak. I felt I was locked in – like a caterpillar in cocoon, only I couldn't find a way out. I was terrified; I thought I'd be stuck like that forever. Thank you Gemma.'

'You should thank Fleabag, he's the one who knew what to do,' Gemma replied, winking at the cat.

Without hesitation, Rowanne reached down and stroked his fur. 'Thank you, she said. 'And I'm sorry I haven't always been fair to you.'

'Apology accepted,' Fleabag purred, 'but only if you keep stroking me.'

Rowanne had lost a great deal of weight, having lived for weeks on sips of soup and water.

Fleabag celebrated the return of his arch-enemy by leading a mountain goat and her kid to their cottage, so they had milk as well as the usual game and fish.

It was not long before Rowanne was up and about,

and taking her share in the daily tasks.

One day, when heavy snow clouds were gathering around the mountain tops, Rowanne and Gemma went to fetch wood. After a while, they came toiling up the steep slope to the cottage dragging a sapling piled high with bundles of firewood. Fleabag jumped onto the wood for the ride. It had been a good afternoon and they were both rosy cheeked and singing loudly as they struggled home.

Hearing the noise, Phelan came out to help, 'What's that black rag you've dragged along?' he teased.

'I'm the King of the Castle!' announced Fleabag as he clung onto the faggots for dear life.

'Get down, you dirty rascal!' laughed the others.

Rowanne wiggled the boughs until Fleabag lost his balance and fell upside down in the snow.

'Is that the way to treat your future king?' he yowled.

'King? *You?*' snorted Rowanne.

Fleabag fluffed up his fur and trotted alongside. 'Little do you know, I've been hiding the Ring under a knot under my chin. Tomorrow I shall produce it and astound you all. Then I'll have your heads cut off for insubordination, then you can all come to my coronation feast.'

'We won't be able to eat much if we've had our

heads cut off!' Rowanne laughed.

'That's the idea, of course. All the more for me.' Fleabag tried a somersault in the air, but it ended up as an upside-down flop. Having completely lost his dignity, the cat chased his tail, spinning round and round and making the snow fly into a small blizzard.

'You know,' Phelan said thoughtfully, 'I think Fleabag ought to be king. He'd make people laugh and forget their worries. Everyone would be happier. Too many people live in fear of Rupert and his henchmen. I'm glad the Ring wasn't found in his palace. He rules by fear and force and that's not what being a king is about.'

Phelan reddened and bowed to Rowanne. 'I'm sorry to insult your betrothed, my lady, but it's true.'

Rowanne went very pale.

Phelan waited, sure she'd lash out at him.

Instead, she breathed deeply. 'You're quite right. While I couldn't speak or move, I did a lot of thinking. I'm so ashamed that I became entangled in Rupert's world. I'm sorry, Phelan – for the way I've treated you, and for what your parents suffered. When we get back, I'd like you to work for me. There are a great many changes needed in Rupertsberg. You know what's most needed there. Will you help?'

Phelan didn't know what to say, so he pretended

he hadn't heard. 'Hurry up,' he called cheerfully, tugging at the wood. 'It's beginning to snow again, let's get this lot into the dry.'

Rowanne stared after him, then called out, 'Phelan, I mean it, *please*?'

Clutching an armful of logs, Phelan turned back. 'I know. Thank you, I'll... I'll have to see.'

That evening Gemma made a venison stew. The onions and turnips they'd bought from the nearest croft were bruised and soft, but the taste was heavenly after a hard day's work. Everyone agreed the gravy needed a good hunk of home-made bread, but that was not to be had, so they drank the juices from their bowls and felt content.

'What will happen when the Ring is found?' asked Gemma. 'Will the finder automatically become the new monarch?'

Rowanne licked her spoon and thought. 'The Fire Wielder told us it will be hidden where only a king or queen would dare to look, so it's unlikely that anyone else would find it. But the Ring'll have to be taken back to the Hall of Light to be formally identified.'

Gemma's face burned, but she said nothing.

'Then the Fire will have to be put back,' Rowanne continued. 'It'll only go into the true Ring, and if the wrong person is holding it, the flame will fade. The Ring doesn't *make* a monarch – it just shows who's the right person.'

'What *is* the Ring Fire?' asked Gemma nervously.

To everyone's surprise, Phelan started to speak. 'It comes from somewhere else – not another planet, just another place. It's alive. Some people say it's the heart of the Fire Giver, reminding us of goodness and truth and all that sort of thing.' He hesitated and shrugged. 'Who knows?'

Rowanne looked at him curiously. 'Where did a thief-lad learn that?'

Phelan hung his head. 'Nowhere,' he mumbled. 'I just heard.' And he gathered up the dishes.

Fleabag broke the uneasy silence that followed. 'When I'm king,' he proclaimed loudly, 'I shall have Gemma prepare my meals. Since she's been in charge of the cooking pot, I've almost gone off mouse.'

'Only almost,' chuckled Gemma, 'I saw you this morning with a particularly fat one for breakfast.'

'That wasn't mouse. That was shrew!' growled Fleabag indignantly. 'When I'm king I'll make a rule about everyone having extra lessons in telling mouse from shrew. Vitally important. Yes, I must make a note of that,' he muttered, as he licked gravy from behind his whiskers.

Then settling into a comfy spot, he wrapped his tail around his nose and went to sleep.

Rowanne was watching Phelan out of the corner of her eye. She could see he was upset and she desperately wanted to make him feel better: 'I meant what I said earlier, you know,' she said. 'I really would like your help to put things right.'

'And I really will think about it,' he replied, and fetched a bowl of water to wash up.

Gemma decided to change the subject. 'Will you marry the Prince, Rowanne?'

'Goodness me, no!' she laughed. 'I knew I wouldn't as soon as he asked me. Although,' she blushed a little, 'I was taken with the idea for a while. All that wealth and power…'

'But if you don't marry him, how will you bring about all these changes you're planning?'

'Ah!' Rowanne winked. 'That's easy. As a close member of the family, I have the right to challenge him for his title.'

'What sort of challenge?'

'It's usually sword fighting or wrestling, but it could be anything, chess or any contest of skill, as long as both sides agree. There are three challenges and you have to win all three to take the title.'

'And if you don't win?' Gemma asked.

Rowanne looked serious. 'If I can't beat an idiot like him, then I don't deserve to rule the city. But if I do win, it'll go back to its old name of Erbwenneth. I'll have none of this Rupertsberg nonsense when I'm princess. And another thing, Queen Sophia can't have known what was happening there – I'm sure she wouldn't have stood for it. I'll invite the monarch for a visit at least once a year.'

'It'll be a pleasure,' came Fleabag's fur-muffled voice from next to the fire.

24 Phelan Turns Back

Once Rowanne was well enough to help with hunting and repairs, Phelan became more and more quiet and withdrawn. The snow was falling thicker and lasted longer. Wolves howled in the mountains after dark.

'Doesn't "Phelan" mean "wolf"?' Rowanne asked one night.

Despite the crackling fire, Phelan shivered. 'Yes, but it's not a name I'd have chosen. Wolves are yet another thing I'm frightened of. My parents gave me a different name, but I can't remember it. I was called Phelan because when I was found, my hair was all matted and I was grey with dirt. I'd been living rough for quite a while.'

'Shall we call you something else?' Gemma asked kindly.

'Like Catslayer?' Rowanne suggested with a twinkle.

'Thank you, but Phelan will do. When I discover who I really am, I might change it, but until then I don't think I'd answer to anything else.'

'What do you mean about discovering who you really are?' Gemma asked.

Phelan shrugged. 'I remember my parents ran a shop that sold second-hand bits and pieces – so I don't think I'm anyone special. Far from it. It's just that when they were killed, I was forced to become someone I'm not. I didn't *like* being a thief but it was the only way I could survive. It was fun at first – being big and brave and macho like the grown ups. But deep down we were all unhappy.

'One of the gang had been a goldsmith, but got involved with a fraud. He knew what he'd done was wrong, but he daren't go back. All that skill wasted. He was utterly miserable and so frustrated.

'Another was a farmer – and a good one by all accounts. He was thrown off his land because Rupert wanted pleasure gardens there! The man had nowhere else to go but the woods. It turned him strange. He'd been a decent bloke once but he became the most vicious and mean of the lot. He was convinced everyone was out to get him and steal the few bits and pieces he'd put together over the years.'

'But what about you, Phelan?' urged Gemma. 'Who would you like to be?'

He shrugged. 'I don't really know. Most of all in the world I'd like a job and friends. I want to be able to live without hurting people.' He thought for a moment. 'I could do something like Aelforth at the hostel, maybe. I'd feel like I was being useful. I'd like that.'

Rowanne was about to make her offer again, but Fleabag twitched his whiskers. Now was not the time. If he wanted to be her steward in Rupertsberg, he'd come when he was ready.

Fleabag jumped into Phelan's lap. 'I'll employ you as tummy scratcher if you like. You'll be paid in dead rats and a fleas, but only when I can spare them!'

Phelan laughed and pushed the incorrigible cat back onto the floor.

Long after the others were asleep, Phelan lay awake thinking. He felt uncomfortable in the company of a knight of the Queen's Guard who wanted him to work for her, a highly intelligent talking cat, and worst of all, someone who carried the Ring Fire.

He didn't *belong* with them. They were special and important. He felt small and out of place.

I must leave, he told himself. *Rowanne is strong again – they don't need me. I'd like to keep an eye on them from a distance, like I did before, but I can't, not in this snow – I won't survive.*

He sighed and looked fondly at each of the

sleeping friends. *It's best if I just go.* He crept to the outside door and looked out. In the silver starlight he could see where the hills became mountains. It was beautiful, but lonely and forbidding as well.

It's very cold and slippery out there, he thought. *I'll slip away at dawn, before the others get up. I'll be safe in a village by nightfall. There's bound to be a farmer somewhere needing extra help. I don't need paying, just food and shelter. I'll move on in spring and get a proper job then.*

He shut the door and sat for a while with the animals. He milked the goat and tried to think while he drank. *What do I need to take with me? I don't have anything – except for the old cloak Rowanne gave me. I'm sure she won't mind me keeping it.*

Then he remembered the deathcap toadstool. He'd left it to dry in a gap in the wall. He slipped that into his pocket. *If I'm caught by wolves, I'll eat it rather than be torn to shreds. They say it works quickly.*

It was still too dark to walk safely, so he went back to the fire and dozed until he was roused by the first pale streaks of light under the door. Phelan stepped softly over the sleeping Gemma and Rowanne, but he had not counted on Fleabag slipping out for a pre-breakfast nibble.

The cat was just washing his paws and talking to Porridge, the more intelligent of the two ponies, when

Phelan stumbled over him.

'Where are you off to?' challenged the cat.

Phelan thought quickly. 'Er... I'm going to ask around the farms to buy hay for the horses. There's no grass worth speaking of now. I thought I'd try and get some flour too. Gemma was saying she missed bread.'

Fleabag picked at a flea and said, 'You'd better take the horse and the pack pony for that lot. How much money did Rowanne give you?'

Bother that cat, thought Phelan, *why does he never mind his own business?*

'Er, oh, I forgot the money.'

Fleabag immediately went to call Rowanne.

Phelan considered just bolting down the hillside, but he wouldn't get far unless he stole a horse, so he stayed.

The inner door creaked open. Rowanne stood there, stiff and bleary-eyed. 'How much do you need?'

From the depths of the cottage Gemma called out, 'A sack of flour and two bales of hay will cost about nineteen groats. If you can buy some vegetables as well, it'd be good, but you might not be lucky. We've bought nearly everything the local crofters have for sale. Give him three silver pieces, Rowanne.'

The knight counted out the money.

Phelan did not want to take it, but he'd been caught

out by his own lie.

Calm down, he told himself. *Once you're out of sight of the cottage, you can stop and think.*

He pocketed the money. 'Gemma's right, the farmers between here and the marshes have scarcely enough to keep themselves alive. I'll ride to one of the larger villages – if I'm not back at nightfall, don't worry.' He saddled the horse and pack pony and led them outside.

It was a glorious morning. The sun was shining in an intensely blue sky. Everything was clean and brilliantly white after another fall of fresh snow. The horses danced a little, glad to be out of the cramped stable. Hiding the turmoil of his feelings, Phelan turned back and waved cheerfully at the others.

The horses picked their way gingerly down to the road below. With one more wave, Phelan turned southward.

Gemma went back inside and sat by the fire. She began to poke at it miserably. Fleabag rubbed his fur against her leg. 'What's the matter?'

'I shouldn't have let him go.'

'Why's that?' asked the cat, jumping into her lap.

'He's miserable. I'm sure he thinks we don't need him and don't want him. I'm scared he won't come back.'

'Are your hands burning?'

'Not yet.'

'Well,' Fleabag stretched out to get the most heat on his tummy fur, 'I suggest you stay just where you are while I have my between-breakfasts doze. Then, if your hands start warning you something's wrong, we'll go and see what's what!' Gemma lifted the cat from her lap onto her blanket. 'Oh, you're useless,' she moaned, and went outside to stare blankly at Phelan's tracks in the snow.

25   Trapped!

Phelan rode for about two miles. Fields and hills lay dazzling white in the brilliant sunshine and the snow had drifted in frozen waves against hedges and walls. Far ahead, the rough land gave way to marshes, then to tamer country and richer farms that might have spare food for sale.

As Phelan rode further and further from the cottage, he began to worry. The others would be depending on these supplies. Could he get them, leave them outside the door, then slip away again? No. Daylight was too short. It couldn't be done before dark and tomorrow he might not have the courage.

Anyway, now Rowanne was strong again, she could go and buy what was needed.

He reined the mare to a halt and looked around. Soon the land would become easier. He could ride fast – faster if he left the pack pony here. If he took her with him she'd slow his progress but, on the other hand, he could sell her. She must be worth something.

He shook his head. 'Stop thinking like that Phelan, you aren't a thief anymore!' he told himself firmly.

Just then, he heard hoofbeats behind him.

Cantering down the road were Rowanne and Fleabag on Porridge. The pony was thoroughly enjoying the run. Her sturdy legs sent clouds of powdery snow high into the sunlit air.

Rowanne waved enthusiastically. 'Wait for us!' she called. Then she caught sight of his miserable face and hesitated. 'I hope you didn't mind us coming. It's such a glorious morning and we gave you so many errands, it didn't seem fair to make you do everything.'

'What she means,' chimed in Fleabag, 'is that she needs to get out of that poky hidy-hole before she screams at someone – probably me.'

Phelan shrugged. Perhaps he ought to play along just for today? They did need a lot of things and if more snow fell, it'd be a long time before they could buy anything else.

Could he live with himself knowing he'd left a carrier of the Ring Fire snowed in with little or no food?

He smiled sheepishly. 'Sorry. Away in my own world. Will Gemma be all right on her own?' Rowanne turned in the saddle and shielded her eyes against the glare of the snow. 'She's coming too. She won't be long, it's not far and it's all downhill.'

Within a few minutes, another black dot came

leaping along the road. Fleabag jumped onto Pudding's back and whispered a few words of horse speech into her ear. Without hesitating the pony clambered back up the slope to meet Gemma.

'Why can that cat make Pudding do as she's told when I can't?' Phelan wondered out loud.

'I suspect he makes terrible threats, probably involving finding new homes for his fleas under her saddlecloth,' Rowanne laughed.

The four of them rode downhill for about an hour. The road was slippery where the snow had thawed and refrozen in patches. The sun was almost warm when they chose a rocky outcrop to eat lunch.

While the others chewed dried meat and laughed at Fleabag's plans for his kingdom, Phelan sat silently surveying the landscape.

Any other day, he'd have said how beautiful everything looked. Today he just measured the distance between himself and the nearest village.

They had left the hills behind and the next stretch of road was stony and full of holes. Crossing that would take another hour or more. Then there was the marshy area with a few tumbledown buildings fairly close to the road on a little rise.

That'll be a good place to aim for when I do run away, Phelan thought. *There might not be food or work, but I can shelter there a night or two.*

Rowanne gave him a friendly prod with the toe of her boot. 'Time to go, we don't want to risk being out after dark.'

Phelan shivered at the thought and jumped down from his rocky perch to where the horses were waiting.

But the snow had an under-layer of ice. As Phelan landed, he slipped, jamming his foot deep into a crack. For a few moments he lay stunned, then slow relentless throbs of pain jabbed through his body.

Rowanne helped him sit. 'Are you all right?'

Gemma knelt by his foot and gently tried to ease it from the cleft.

'Ow!' Phelan gasped.

Gemma reached down and loosened the thongs that tied his boot. 'Wriggle your foot out, we'll get the shoe afterwards.'

But it did not help. For almost an hour, they tugged at his leg until the pain became unbearable.

Rowanne pulled out her dagger. Using the tip, she gouged some of the looser chunks of rock away, and snapped the blade. 'Bother! I'll go on to the next farm and see if I can borrow a hammer or a crowbar – preferably both. It'll be nightfall soon and we don't want to get caught here. I've seen a lot of tracks in the snow; I fear the wolves are running low.'

'Well, tell them from me that the cat is running high!' replied Fleabag, fluffing out his chest fur. 'I was known as "Wolfbane" in my youth!'

Gemma scowled at him. 'This isn't funny. You go Rowanne, I'll stay with Phelan.'

'So will I,' added Fleabag. 'He might need someone to protect him.'

'I can't think of anyone more useless in a spot,' Rowanne jibed. 'You're all quips – and no equipment!'

Fleabag pretended that he hadn't heard, but his tail twitched irritably.

'Come on, cat!' called Gemma. 'Help me find firewood. We won't go far and it'll help us keep warm!'

All alone, Phelan sat still and closed his eyes. He couldn't help imagining snarling wolves, saliva dripping from yellow fangs.

Phelan's breath tightened and he began to wheeze. 'Think of something else,' he told himself. 'Open your eyes.' But it didn't help. Heavy clouds were blowing in from across the mountains.

All he could think about was wolves.

Then a chilling thought made him shudder. 'If I were dead, the others would be free to leave me and go home. I don't want to die, but if I can save them, then I must do it.'

He felt in his pocket for the deadly toadstool.

Nothing.

He rummaged in the other pocket. Still nothing...

'I know I put it in,' he muttered to himself. 'I remember doing it. Did I drop it? Please, no... If someone thought it was a shrivelled mushroom and put it in the pot for tonight's supper...'

He gulped and shook his head. He had to think more positively. 'I dropped it and it's gone. That's all. I'm well and truly trapped. There's no way to escape. Bother the others being so kind. They're bound to insist on staying with me. When night falls, the wolves will get us all.'

Phelan shivered. He was getting very cold. Even his thick cloak was no real protection from the wind. The sunlight had gone and snow clouds were piling high. His body throbbed and burned with ice and fear.

He wriggled forward and examined his ankle. He had hoped if he stayed still, that the swelling would go down so he could ease his foot out. His toes still moved, so nothing was broken. If he could get free, they all stood a chance.

Taking a handful of snow, he rubbed it as far down his leg as he could reach to reduce any swelling. But his skin ached and his foot remained as stuck as ever.

The wind was whipping up. If the wolves didn't get him, the cold would. 'I must keep warm,' he decided. 'For the others' sakes, I must fight, it's the only way.' He swung his arms wildly and slapped himself all over.

Once more he searched his pockets, vainly hoping that amongst the dusty lint and bits of string there might be something useful. Nothing.

Closing his eyes, Phelan fought his fears. 'I must think of something good,' he muttered, remembering the Ring Fire dancing in Gemma's hand. That helped.

But if the Ring isn't found, the Fire will fade, he realised. *That'll mean the end of hope. There'll be utter misery throughout the land. Without it, everyone will feel as empty and desolate as I do now.*

The Ring must be found so the Fire can make sure a good monarch sits on the throne. Without it, there'll be war and tyrants everywhere.

'If I get out of this alive,' he said aloud, 'I'll stay with my friends and help them find the Ring. Even something as ordinary as helping them survive the winter or fighting off robbers is important. I may be a common thief, but for once, I'm going to be someone who *acts*, instead of running away all the time.'

He pulled his cloak more tightly around his shoulders and wished the others were back. Brave decisions needed brave friends.

It was not long before he heard Gemma and Fleabag cheerfully poking fun at each other as they hauled sticks and brushwood back to where he sat.

Wolves were frightened of fire.

Phelan helped to snap the wood into kindling while Gemma went back to gather more. He selected a few strong, straight branches and rubbed the ends against the rock until they had sharp points. At a pinch these could be jabbed at an animal's eyes. He would fight as long as he was able to.

Wolves could smell fear in a man's sweat. If he thought about the Ring Fire, he might not smell too bad and they might not come. *For once in my life,* Phelan told himself firmly, *I am not going to be afraid.*

26   Wolf Pack

The sound of howling mingled with the whistle of the wind in the foothills behind them. The beginnings of yet another blizzard yellowed the sky and the daylight faded into unhappy greyness.

Rowanne bowed before the blast, clutching her cloak around her as she led the mare by the head. The horse stumbled through the ever-deepening snow. Bundled on the animal's back were faggots of wood collected on the way.

The crofter had given Rowanne short shrift, refusing to lend or sell tools of any kind. Now the friends were left with nothing but their wits to keep themselves alive through the night.

Painfully cold, Rowanne struggled back to where the others huddled together under their cloaks. The two ponies had been tethered under a small overhang – not close enough to share warmth, but one good fire should keep the wolves away from them all.

To Rowanne's surprise, although there was a good pile of wood ready, it was left cold and wet, with the snow-dappled figures shivering miserably around it.

'Thank goodness you're here,' mewed Fleabag pitifully. 'Phelan forgot to bring a tinderbox and Gemma's hands are raw from trying to light the wood with a spindle.'

'I'll be with you in a minute.' Rowanne threw her wood down and led her horse to shelter with the others. When she returned, Gemma pulled a few bits of dry kindling from under her cloak.

Just then, the sound of snuffling made the horses stamp and whinny in terror.

'Light the fire!' urged Fleabag. 'Quickly!'

The first sparks from Rowanne's tinderbox failed, but soon a small flicker grew – and the bright golden eyes of a young wolf reflected the flames.

Rowanne wound her handkerchief around a stick, lit it then jabbed it into the animal's face. With a whimper it turned tail and ran into the blizzard.

Returning to the fire, Rowanne coaxed a few larger twigs alight until there was a small but comforting blaze. 'Keep it going,' she told Phelan. 'I'm going to see to the horses.'

A few minutes later, she carried the saddles back to the fireside. 'Here,' she gave one to Gemma. 'It'll be warmer sitting on this than ice-cold stone.'

Phelan could not manage the saddle, but Rowanne found a log to slide under his backside.

'My ears are cold,' moaned the cat.

'You'll be nice and snug in a wolf's tummy in a minute,' muttered Rowanne, 'Try sorting out small twigs. That'll keep you warm.'

Gemma pulled a nicely burning stick from the fire and peered around for more wolves. Holding the torch high, she let its yellow light toss in the wind. Then a snow-laden gust doused the flame.

A few strides to the left, the silhouette of a wolf sniffed at the dying smoke. It hesitated, then sank low and crept forwards.

Drawing her sword, Rowanne lunged, dispatched the animal cleanly and flung the carcass downhill. 'The smell of blood will bring the whole pack now.'

'Do they feed on their own kind?' Phelan asked.

She shrugged as she cleaned her blade. 'I have no idea. Let's hope so, or they'll be after human, horse – or even cat-flesh before long.'

The dusk was deepening. Out of the darkness slunk more musty-smelling shadows. The fire seemed to be losing the struggle for life in the teeth of the cold and wet. One by one, the tiny flames winked yellow, orange, then red as they cooled and died.

Phelan leaned sideways, holding his cloak as a shelter from the wind. But it was not enough.

Gemma's benumbed fingers struggled again and

again as she tried to light the last few dry wood-shavings. 'It's no good!' She flung it down, almost crying. 'The kindling just won't catch!'

'Let me have a go,' offered Phelan. 'Hold the cloak up, will you?'

For several minutes he struggled. 'Everything's too wet. I can't even get a smoulder.'

Irritably, Rowanne snatched the tinder box. 'Here, let me do it.'

'Hurry, the wolves are almost on us.' Gemma urged through chattering teeth.

'Pooh, they stink!' Fleabag moaned. 'And they sound hungry. Get that fire going.'

'Don't rush me!' Rowanne snapped, slamming stone and metal together. She caught her knuckles, yelped, then both flint and steel rattled into the crevice under Phelan's foot.

'Oh!' she gasped. 'I'm so sorry!' She lay flat on her stomach and groped down the black crack. It was too dark to see anything; even the intense white of the snow had faded into an endless grey smudge of whirling flakes.

Fleabag pushed his paw down the hole. 'It's too deep for me,' he mewed miserably.

Phelan tried again. 'I can touch it, but I can't pick it up.'

'I'll have a go,' offered Gemma. 'I've got the smallest hands.' She reached into the crack with achingly cold fingers. 'Sorry, I can't even feel it.' She sat up and wrapped her throbbing hand in the folds of her cloak. She longed for the comforting warmth of the Ring Fire.

No one snapped at Rowanne – although they all longed to.

The knight pulled a small flask of spiced cordial from her pocket and passed it around in silence.

'Why don't you three ride back to the cottage?' urged Phelan, trying to be brave. 'You still stand a chance if you go back now, but none at all if you stay.'

'We couldn't do it in this dark and snow,' Rowanne replied. 'If I'd realized earlier on in the day just how difficult this was going to be, I'd have gone back for all sorts of things – like food.'

Gemma's stomach rumbled at the thought. 'I'd give anything for a bowl of hot soup,' she murmured, squeezing her aching hands under her armpits.

'I think we all would,' Rowanne agreed. She was glad no one could see how worried she felt. She was a trained knight. She had been sent to protect Gemma. Survival was her responsibility, and she was failing. 'Who has weapons of any kind?' she asked.

'My claws are the sharpest in the kingdom,'

Fleabag announced proudly. 'They have put out the eyes of many of the Queen's foes!'

'I've sharpened some sticks,' offered Phelan. 'If we sort through the firewood for the strongest branches, we could make some more. Has anyone got a knife?'

Rowanne handed him the broken dagger blade. 'Sharpening wood is about all it's fit for now,' she said, peering into the deepening gloom where the dark shapes seemed to be multiplying.

The beasts were crouching, waiting...

As the scent of wolf grew stronger, Porridge whinnied and tugged at her halter. Gemma got up and straightened the rug on the pony's back, talking gently to all the time. It crossed her mind that if she took the rug, it might help keep Rowanne and Phelan warmer. But she couldn't do it. Poor Porridge was shivering with cold and terror as it was.

And should they find a way to free Phelan's foot, the ponies needed to be warm and well to escape from the wolves. Gemma smoothed her face against the animal's neck. The scent of hay in Porridge's mane made her feel better. For a while she stayed quite still. Perhaps they could all take turns to warm up like this during the night? It might keep them going – except for poor old Phelan.

Reluctantly she left the horses to return to the

others. But as she turned, a lithe shape darted between herself and her friends.

Crouching low, the animal snarled at Gemma, steering her back to where she'd be caught between high rocks behind her and a sheer drop to her left. The heavy smell of wet wolf hair mixed with foul breath as the beast closed in.

Gemma glanced around in panic. 'Rowanne!' she whispered, too frightened to scream. 'Rowanne! *Help*!'

But the howling wind carried her words away.

The mare whinnied and shied, lashing out at the wolf with her hooves. Porridge and Pudding did the same. But they were too well tethered to do any good.

The noise roused Rowanne from her icy state of near-exhaustion. She leapt up, sword in hand. Swiping left and right, she injured a few wolves, but it was too dark to see properly.

Fleabag sprang forwards, hissing. His ears flattened, his whiskers spread and his fur bristled, but all his bravado did no good, for between Gemma and her friends was a semicircle of deadly hunters, merciless and hungry.

Gemma took a step or two to the right. The wolves swayed that way too. Then she crept back. The musty bodies crowded closer.

The horses tugged at their ropes, rolling their eyes and screaming. Rowanne bellowed and lunged once more at the attackers. Phelan flung the first of his wooden spears in the opposite direction.

They were surrounded.

Gemma froze with horror. The wolves had succeeded in separating the travellers from each other.

None of them could help anyone else.

Pudding howled in pain. Yellow fangs sank into her leg, or perhaps it was her neck. Who knew?

Anyway, it was too late.

27 The Burning

Gemma was angry.

Flinging her arms wide, she yelled, '*Go away!*' and stamped on the snow-covered rock.

From her hands, great plumes of orange and yellow fire streaked into the night sky.

Rowanne and Phelan watched open-mouthed.

With howls of dismay, the whole pack of wolves turned and ran into the night.

The snow stopped falling and the Ring Fire faded.

Now the darkness was everywhere, pressing in on them with a heavy silence from which there seemed to be no escape.

Shaking with fear and astonishment, Gemma grabbed Phelan's hand. 'W-was that the R-ring Fire?' she whispered.

'It was,' he replied, squeezing her icy fingers. 'You did well.'

A few clouds blew aside, letting the moonlight through. Fleabag ventured out from under the blanket and pawed at Gemma's trouser leg. 'You're shaking. Come in the warm,' he mewed. 'I'll go and make sure Pudding's all right.'

'I'll help,' Rowanne offered, feeling a little unsteady herself.

In the silvery light they could see the pony only had a shoulder wound. Rowanne packed clean snow around it to staunch the blood. 'She'll be fine if she's not attacked again.'

Using more snow, the knight wiped the wolf-blood from her sword. She dried the blade carefully on her cloak, then slipped it back into its scabbard.

The sudden burst of Fire had unsettled her, she needed to be doing things, so she turned her attention to the carcasses scattered across the frozen ground. 'Gemma,' she called, 'Help me shift some of these beasts away, will you? I don't want the smell of blood to lure the pack back.'

There was no answer.

'Gemma, I need help, *please*,' Rowanne was getting cross.

Phelan replied, 'I think you'd better come up here.'

Muttering crossly, Rowanne stomped uphill towards their camp, but once again, clouds blew across the moon. 'Where are you?' she shouted. 'I can't see.'

'Over here,' Phelan's voice beckoned.

After a lot of slipping and swearing, the knight reached the rock where Phelan was trapped. She groped forward until she touched the remains of the bonfire.

'Stand back,' came Gemma's voice. 'Well away from the wood.'

'Why? What's happened?'

'It's just that...' Gemma ventured, 'well, if... if I can make fire come, like *that*... Then why shouldn't I light *this* fire?'

Rowanne held her breath and stared wide-eyed.

Tentatively, Gemma stretched out her hands towards the kindling and thought hard about heat. But nothing happened. She screwed her eyes tightly closed. 'Come on, Ring Fire!' she said. '*Burn!*'

She could hear the nervous, quiet breathing of the others – but no crackle or snap, no warmth or smell of burning. She opened her eyes and stared into the darkness. The snow had a pale luminescence, but that was all.

There was no Ring Fire.

Angry and embarrassed, she said nothing, but snuggled between her two friends and tried to go to sleep. Numbing cold had taken her limbs and she was exhausted.

'Never mind, Gemma,' Phelan said kindly, giving Gemma a hug. 'You tried.'

The pitch-black, colder-than-ice dead of night wore on. The four of them sat almost silently, taking turns to comfort the horses or move around a little. Phelan whittled at sticks to make more improvised spears until he could hold the broken dagger no longer.

Occasionally a shadow shifted, or they heard a slight scuffle or snarl. The wolves still waited in the dark, although further away than before.

From time to time, Rowanne took up Gemma's spindle and socket to try to revive the fire. But apart from a slight whiff of smoke, nothing happened. They shared the last of the food and spiced cordial.

The long hours dragged.

At last Gemma managed to doze, and she dreamed about the Ring Fire in a way that was real enough to actually feel heat. 'Mustn't,' she mumbled to herself, 'that's how people go when they are dying of cold – they think they're warm.'

'No,' Phelan whispered back, shaking her gently. 'It's real. We *are* warm, look.'

Gemma forced herself to wake up.

Fleabag yawned and stretched. 'What did you do that for?' he moaned.

'What?'

'You put the fire out, just as my paws were thawing.'

'What's everyone talking about?' Gemma asked, rubbing her eyes.

Fleabag nuzzled his warm furry nose against Gemma's face. 'You lit the fire, then you put it out!'

Suddenly she realized she really *had* been warm. 'But how could I?' she asked nervously.

'Just now,' Rowanne began, 'while you were sitting quite still, there was a fire by your feet. It wasn't the bonfire – no twigs or anything, just fire. But then you stirred and sat up, and it was gone!' She clicked her fingers. 'Like blowing a candle out.'

Gemma shook her head. 'You're dreaming.'

Below the rock, a wolf shadow shifted closer.

'Go on,' urged Fleabag. 'Think of the Ring Fire again.'

With a pounding heart, Gemma opened her hands. A tiny glowing light budded between her fingers.

Then it grew, bigger and bigger.

Very gingerly, Gemma carried the precious golden flame to the pile of wood. 'Please, burn,' she said quietly, 'or we're all wolf meat.'

With a soft roar, the wood caught. Orange flames leaped high into the night sky. With a cheery crackling and hissing, heat and light challenged the darkness.

Flying sparks caught in shaggy coats. The wolves howled and ran.

Rowanne and Fleabag stared in amazement and awe at Gemma.

She stared back at them, gaunt and shaking. 'Did *I* do that?' she whispered.

For a long while, no one spoke.

Then Phelan said softly, 'The Ring Fire did it – you just allowed it to happen.'

'But why didn't it do it before?'

'Because you wanted it to obey you. You were trying to force it, as if you were a wizard. It's the sort of thing the Chancellor would have done. The Ring Fire obeys no one. It burns when someone allows it to do so, not when people try to *make* it happen.'

Gemma closed her eyes and remembered the Fire Wielder in the Hall of Light, giving the last bit of his strength to enable the Ring Fire to burn even though it was separated from the royal Ring.

'It burns where it is welcome,' the Fire Wielder had told her.

Gemma turned to Phelan, wide-eyed. He did not look happy. Caught as he was by his foot, he couldn't run or turn away.

'How *do* you know so much?' she asked gently.

There was another long silence. Phelan looked thoughtfully into the firelight. When he spoke, his voice was taut. 'When I said no one would take me in after my parents died, it wasn't true. I lived with Aelforth at the Rupertsberg hostel for a while and he did his best. He is a wise man. He understands things like the Ring Fire.

'But I made friends with street kids who were learning to be thieves and pick-pockets. I wanted to be big and tough like them, not quiet and gentle like Aelforth. So I ran away and lived rough until I could prove myself as a thief – then they took me in. But I really was grey and filthy. That part was no lie!'

He smiled as he watched the living gold flames. 'Since then I've done a lot of running away. But if I get out of this I promise I'll stay and help as best I can.'

As if approving of his words, the fire crackled, then roared, sending dancing sparks into the night sky.

Phelan leaned his head on his knees and sat quite still until dawn.

As first light crept across the snow to the east, the flames died and the friends stirred and stretched.

It was then Phelan gasped, 'I don't believe it!' He wiggled his foot free, and stood up.

Before the sun had fully risen, the companions had

saddled the horses and were well on their way home. The wind had dropped and there was no more snow, but the journey took almost three hours because of the uphill climb.

Gemma sagged on the pony's back and didn't speak the whole way. As soon as they were inside their tiny cottage, she sank into a corner and curled up by a very ordinary fire – lit with Phelan's tinderbox.

Rowanne tended the horses then lay down beside Gemma and slept.

Wrapped in a blanket with Fleabag asleep on his lap, Phelan sat on the doorstep and stared at the endless snow. He wasn't cold; something bright was burning inside him. 'I'm sorry,' he whispered softly, 'I won't run away again.'

It was late in the afternoon when Phelan roused them all with a bowl of hot broth.

Rowanne thanked him. 'That smells good. How's your ankle? Are you all right? Any frostbite?

He shook his head. 'It's funny, but I haven't felt this well for years. I'm sort of – *me* again' His eyes glinted. 'I can't tell you how good it feels.'

Still half asleep in a corner, Gemma smiled. She was glad he was happy. She wished she felt the same; but everything that happened with the Ring Fire the night before had terrified her.

She ate the broth and slept again.

Two days later there was a lull in the biting northerly wind. Rowanne and Phelan went down to the plain together to buy the hay, flour and vegetables they needed for the long weeks ahead.

Phelan said almost nothing the whole way. As they approached the place where the burning had happened, he reined in Pudding, and stared at the spot for a long time.

'Gemma doesn't want to believe she's carrying the Ring Fire, does she?' he asked.

Rowanne bought her mare alongside. 'No,' she replied tersely, urging her horse on. She wasn't sure whether she hated or loved what was happening. One thing was clear; Gemma was more than just a street brat who'd identify the real Ring when she saw it.

And she, the Lady-Knight Rowanne de Montiland, was jealous. *All is not lost,* she told herself. *I still might find the Ring – or be present when it's found. Anyway, without me, none of them will survive.*

Pushing her feelings aside, Rowanne concentrated on keeping to the muddy path.

28   The Warming

Spring arrived suddenly and joyously just two weeks later. Out in the sunshine, Phelan leaned his back against the cottage wall. His skin glowed like dark honey and his black hair curled over his shoulders. He smiled contentedly to himself, then waved as Gemma passed by with a bucket. 'Do you need a hand?'

'No thank you. I'll be fine,' she replied.

Once he thought he was alone, Phelan took a deep breath, closed his eyes and began to sing:

'Spring is here and snow-blossom's falling
on grass as green as my lady's gown.
Hope is here and birds are singing
by field and flock, and byre and burn.

> *The wheel, the wheel, the wheel is turning*
> *Blessed the warmth of the Ring Fire's burning...'*

His rich voice filled the warm air.

By the stream, Gemma put the pail down and stood transfixed. The song brought a lump to her throat. Slowly she crept closer and listened as each verse unfurled like a fern leaf.

Fleabag padded out to sit by Phelan's feet. For once, he made no rude quips.

When the song was finished, Phelan opened his eyes and laughed at Gemma, who was staring at him, her mouth open like a trout.

Coming to herself, she wiped her eyes and went inside. The song made her feel as if she was hearing the Ring Fire speak again.

But the words made Gemma feel uncomfortable. Every little reminder that she was carrying the Fire worried her. *I'm too small for something this big, she thought. Yet Phelan seems to like it; since the night with the wolves, he's changed, he's become settled and happy.*

Trying to ignore it, she busied herself with every little task she could find and did several things twice – – but the words of Phelan's song still turned and turned inside her head.

The next day, Fleabag patted Gemma's leg with his paw. 'Come with me,' he purred. 'I've got some fleas I can't quite reach, can you help please?'

'Of course.' Gemma found his comb, but the cat wriggled out of reach.

'In private please. I don't like Rowanne's sneering. I can't help having hitch hikers.'

It was a chilly day, but Fleabag led Gemma outside

to a sheltered spot in the lee of the woodpile. 'Make yourself comfy,' he said, then he jumped onto her lap.

But instead of rolling on his back and purring so she could work through his tummy fur, he sat bolt upright and fixed Gemma with his golden stare.

'Right,' he said sternly. 'Spill the beans. What's the matter?'

'Nothing,' Gemma replied, tugging at a knot on his shoulder. 'You'll have to come closer, I can't comb you if you don't co-operate.'

'And I can't help *you* if *you* don't co-operate!'

'You can't help me anyway,' she replied flatly.

'Who says?' Fleabag blinked at her.

Gemma raked the comb through the cat's tangled ruff. 'You don't seem to have many fleas.'

'Course I haven't. I ate them all for breakfast. I just wanted to get you alone.'

Gemma flung the comb down crossly. 'So, why am I out here in this chilly wind? So you can eat me too?'

He blinked.

Gemma tried to push the cat off, but he dug his claws into her knee.

'Stop it and listen!' he said firmly. 'You are unhappy. A blind, half-witted field mouse could see that, even if he looked out of his hole backwards.'

Folding her arms, Gemma stared at the sky.

The cat wasn't going to give up. 'You're upset about the Ring Fire? So tell me what you're feeling, because none of this is going to go away.'

Gemma shrugged. 'It's just that... Well... You, of all people should understand. After all, you're like me – we're both strays. We came from nowhere and after this is done, we're *going* nowhere. Or so I thought. Suddenly I seem to have been given the most important thing in the whole world to carry.'

She fell silent.

'And?' Fleabag nuzzled her chin.

Gemma sighed. 'I could cope with being little Gemma Streetchild who had to go on an errand for her queen. But now, it's all become too big. I don't like it. It's too much to ask of someone like me.'

Fleabag ignored a dormouse that scuttled past. 'Who *says* you're only Gemma Streetchild?' he demanded. 'Who *says* I'm only a mangy old street cat that a queen tolerated in her palace? No one in the whole wide world is "only" anything. I have heard that one day the Fire will be given to *everyone* to carry – then we won't need queens and laws, because we'll all act kindly and sensibly. Won't that be nice?'

Gemma laughed bitterly. 'If only it were true.'

She hadn't noticed Phelan coming quietly round the woodpile. She jumped as he knelt on a log next to them. 'Let the Ring Fire burn, Gemma.'

She winced. 'Now?'

'Yes. Let it burn a little. It'll help us all not to be afraid.'

'Of what?' Gemma bit her lip.

'You're afraid to be who you are... aren't you?'

Heart thumping, Gemma opened her fingers into a cup and watched as the tiny flame flickered there.

Everyone was silent for a long moment.

'It's funny,' Gemma said at last, her head on one side, 'I'd had always thought of it as burning for right or wrong, or for getting rid of horrid things – but I never realized before how good it is just to look at. It makes me feel as if everything'll be all right.'

That afternoon the weather turned cold again. Their shelter felt very cramped and tempers became frayed.

Rowanne became increasingly officious and Fleabag took great delight in winding her up.

But Phelan and Gemma sat with the horses and talked. He told her everything he could remember about the Ring Fire and she told him about the queen, how kind and good she was and how she'd have been angry if she'd seen the injustice of Rupertsberg, or the neglect and poverty around Porthwain.

'Queen Sophia knew she was too old to rule,'

Gemma explained. 'She longed to find a good successor. I wonder how *she* was chosen?'

Phelan considered for a while, then he shook his head. 'It must've been a long time ago, when she was very young. I don't know what she did – but I expect it was very special.'

'The Fire Wielder told me the Ring would be hidden where only a king or queen would dare to look.' Gemma remembered. 'Queen Sophia said everyone at the festival was so busy trying to do noble feats, they were missing the point of what being a monarch was all about.'

She hesitated, then asked, 'What'll they do if no one is found? What if the Ring is lost for ever?'

Phelan twisted a wisp of straw into a knot and pulled it tight. 'Rowanne says things will get dangerous if no one comes forward within a year and a day. The Prime Minister's as old as the Fire Wielder, so when they die, there'll be no one left to prevent wars between the noble families of the six provinces.'

'But what will happen to the Fire? Will it really be given to everybody?'

'Who knows?' Phelan shrugged. 'Aelforth told me that without the Ring, the Fire fades back where it came from.' He paused. 'But it's got to be all right in the end. The Fire Giver would never desert us.'

Gemma sighed. 'The Fire Wielder said he was ready to go to the Quiet Place too. I wonder if he'll still be alive when we get back?'

The wisp of straw snapped in Phelan's fingers. 'If he's not, then everything will be a big mess.'

'I really am glad you're with us,' Gemma said. 'I'm certain that one day you will find out who you really are. Do you think you'll work for Rowanne?'

'I'm sure she means well, but no. I'll think of something. What about you? I can't see you going back to the kitchens.'

Gemma bit her lip. 'No – I don't want to see Cook ever again. Fleabag will be all right. He always is.'

Phelan chuckled. 'It must be nice being a cat. You have to fend for yourself, it's true, but there's usually a bowl of milk and a fireside that'll welcome you – if you can stand the taste of rat, that is.'

'If Rowanne doesn't win the Princedom of Rupertsberg, she could go back to being a knight at court. It suits her. Being cooped up all winter with a talking cat, a thief and a guttersnipe must be miserable for her.'

'It's pretty miserable for us too,' Phelan retorted.

One morning, the companions woke to the sound of a steady dripping noise.

Fleabag ran outside and returned a little later with wet paws and a large fish.

'It's a thaw!' he declared gleefully. 'The trout are swimming and birds are singing. Spring's back – properly this time!'

They led the horses out to graze, and everyone's spirits rose. Even the higher slopes were green.

When breakfast was eaten, Gemma and Fleabag sat on the sun-warmed grass watching early bees searching for blossom. High in the air, an eagle soared, and the earth smelled rich and loamy.

From behind them came a strident voice, 'No lolling; time to be on the move!'

They turned to see Rowanne, arms folded across her leather jerkin and dark hair tucked into the woollen snood she wore under her helmet. 'If we leave straight away and don't get sidetracked, we'll in Harflorum by May, just before the year and a day is up.'

Gemma jumped to her feet. 'But we can't, we need to be close by when the Ring is found.'

Rowanne rolled her eyes. 'And how are you going to do that? You can't watch everyone everywhere. Come *on* Gemma; be sensible. The chances are that some stupid ploughboy dug up the Ring last week and he's already been crowned.'

'I... I don't think so,' Gemma replied with a worried frown.

The knight ignored her. She was staring across the marshes to the plains and the way they had come. 'Get packed, we're going back this morning,' she announced.

Gemma stamped and lifted her chin defiantly. 'No! We go *on*. North by northwest.'

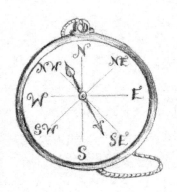

29   Dire Warnings

Rowanne stared at Gemma. 'How can you even think of going on? It took six months to get from Harflorum to where we are now; there're only about nine or ten weeks left of the year and a day. We'll be back in good time if we turn back now. I know you meant well going north by northwest, but we haven't had so much as a sniff of the Ring. No sightings, not even rumours.'

Gemma climbed on a low rock so she could look Rowanne in the eye. 'I know I'm a nobody, but I've done what the Ring Fire said, and I will *keep* doing it. By the oath you swore in Harflorum, you can leave us whenever you like, but I'm going north by northwest until I can go no further. Alone if I have to.'

The girl reddened and her green eyes blazed.

Rowanne blinked, quite taken aback. 'But... but you can't,' she protested. 'You'll be needed at the palace to identify the real Ring. What happens if you don't get back in time?'

Fleabag's ears flattened and he hissed loudly.

Rowanne glared down at him. 'What do *you* want?'

The cat prowled around Rowanne in circles, his tail fluffed up. 'It's what *you* want that worries me – you haven't found the Ring – so do you want to be around when the king or queen is proclaimed so you get yourself a good position at court?'

Rowanne's cheeks flamed.

Fleabag growled up at her. 'I'm right, aren't I?'

'N-no!' Rowanne protested.

'Furthermore,' Fleabag went on, 'you know that without Gemma, there'll be no proclamation at all, because the Fire Wielder might not be alive – maybe she carries the only Ring Fire that's left? You're scared of missing out, that's why you want her with you.'

Rowanne glowered under her dark brows. She pointed a firm finger straight at the cat. 'I have sworn to have your pelt for a collar, and by all I hold precious, one day I will keep that vow!'

Fleabag smirked. 'I'd like to see you try!'

Just then Phelan came outside. 'What's all the noise about?'

Gemma and Rowanne both started talking at once.

Phelan turned to Fleabag. 'Will you come for a stroll? I'll get more sense out of *you*.' And together they wandered towards the stream.

When they returned, Gemma and Rowanne had all their things spread out on the grass. They were sorting and packing furiously in deadly silence.

Phelan stood watching them for a few seconds, then he said, 'I'm going with Gemma.'

'So am I,' added the cat, sitting on Gemma's bag to make his point.

Gemma straightened, clutching a pile of clothes in her arms. 'Rowanne, we need you. The quest for the Ring needs you. Please don't leave us.'

The knight stopped packing and stared at the friends. At last she sighed and bowed her head. 'Very well, I've seen you holding the Ring Fire, Gemma. It's my duty to stay with you. If we start today we may have enough time to get a little further – however, money is getting short. If we don't find the Ring very soon, you must allow me to spend the last of the gold on a swift horse and gallop back to Harflorum. As a Queen's Guard I have also sworn to defend the peace of this kingdom. There'll be trouble when a year and a day are up – I guarantee it. The Fire will lead you as it will, but I must return to the palace. You'll be penniless and on your own. I can do no more.'

'How long have we got?' Phelan asked.

Rowanne used her broken dagger to scratch a calendar on a rock. 'On the vernal equinox, I must turn back. That's about ten days.'

'Good. We agree. Now, which way do we go?'

asked Gemma, sitting on a bundle so Phelan could tie it more tightly.

'On through the mountains,' Rowanne replied, lashing a roll of blankets onto Pudding's pannier. 'I talked to one of the crofters the other day. He reckons the pass will be open by now and it's not a bad road that leads straight to the province of Beulothin. Apparently they have a spectacular Spring Festival,

'How far does north by northwest go on for?' Gemma.

'Beulothin extends from the mountains to the sea. There's nothing else after that, unless you take a ship.' Rowanne stopped tugging at buckles and narrowed her eyes. 'You're still convinced that's the way to go? How long will you keep going?'

'The Ring Fire will tell her when to stop,' Fleabag replied.

Gemma smiled uncertainly. 'Sometimes I feel as if I'm going on forever, but I'm keeping my promise to the queen. I wish the Ring Fire would speak to me again.'

'That's because you need to let the Ring Fire burn *inside* you, not just in your hands,' Phelan said.

Gemma squinted back at him. 'What?'

'Sorry, nothing,' Phelan muttered. Now was not the time for difficult explanations.

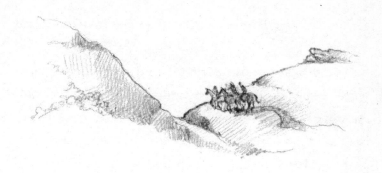

The travellers were soon on the mountain road, but their progress was slowed by patchy ice and snow. The first evening they crested the foothills where they had wintered. The second night it rained and they shivered under a canopy of blankets at the top of the pass. No one slept and they found nothing to eat.

Miserably, they set off again very early. The road wound tortuously between rockfalls and mountain streams. Before noon the path dipped steeply downward, then twisted out of a steep-sided rift until a misty plain spread out far below them.

As the next day wore on, the air warmed. They crossed fertile farmland edged with thick forests. The land was good. Passers-by assured them that the city of Beriot was not far – north by northwest.

'I'm so excited,' Gemma almost bounced in her saddle. 'I am so sick of eating pigeon and rabbit. You know, more than anything I'd like a toasted cheese sandwich. And just think; the city is the right direction. We're close to the Ring, I can feel it.'

The villages became bigger and wealthier. People were busy draping garlands from windows and hanging bunting across the streets. Yet the people did not seem excited. In fact they looked terrified, scuttling between the houses and shops. At the sight of the travellers they turned their backs.

One evening, a friendly farmer's wife fed them well and provided clean, soft beds. The breakfast was particularly splendid with sausages, bacon, fresh bread and golden butter. Fleabag was given a dish of cream.

The woman seemed kind, but like everyone else, she was very sad. As she cleared away the plates, she asked them where they were going.

'We've come to see the Spring Festival,' replied Phelan enthusiastically. 'We've heard it's really exciting.'

The woman pulled herself straight and wrinkled her brow. 'Don't!' she said tersely. 'Go back where you've come from as fast as you can.'

'But why?' Phelan asked in amazement.

She leaned her knuckles on the table and scowled. 'It's a bad business. This is no place for those who don't belong. Come to the *last* day of the festival, if you must – the day of the equinox, when there'll be parties and rejoicing. But for now, if you value your lives, take my advice and *flee!* Clutching a tea towel, she wiped away a tear.

'But what's *wrong*?' Phelan asked.

The woman clicked her tongue and clattered the last of the plates together, but said nothing.

Phelan paid her for their board and lodging and tried to coax more information out of her with an extra silver piece.

Although she looked hungrily at the coin, her mouth was firmly shut.

Bemused, they gathered up their things, loaded the horses and set off.

Fleabag jumped onto Porridge's withers in front of Gemma. 'Something is very wrong here,' he said. 'You've seen how miserable and frightened everyone is? The animals are just as bad. Do you think we should turn back?'

Gemma shrugged. 'I can't, but I won't mind if you want to.'

'If I were king,' muttered Phelan as a man pulled his child inside a house as they approached, 'I'd put this place right first. Perhaps even before Rupertsberg. Something very strange is going on.'

They reached the city of Beriot late that afternoon.

They found a smart looking inn and Rowanne ordered a good meal and a night's lodging for them all. 'This is our final treat,' she said. 'We'll have to sleep rough after this – I've got to keep the last of the money to buy a really good horse to return next week. You can sell my mare for what you can, she's sound, but not very fast.'

The savour of hot pie and roast potatoes filled the dining room. A lanky youth pushed through the crowds with a trolley laden with enough food for twice their company. He stopped by their table.

'Compliments of the management,' he said, with a worried look.

Rowanne caught the lad in her iron grip. 'What do you mean, boy?'

'Nothing to pay, ma'am. The landlord says so. *Ow!*'

Rowanne squeezed his arm. 'Landlords don't give away food to complete strangers. What's happening?'

Just then she caught a glimpse of a fat man in a white apron peering at them.

Rowanne let the boy go. 'That looks very nice indeed, thank you,' she said loudly. 'Will you bring me some pepper?'

The lad scurried off and returned quickly with a small earthenware pot.

As he put it in front of her, he whispered, 'Please,

my lady as soon as you've eaten, go back where you came from.'

Rowanne grabbed for the child again, but he'd darted away.

Gemma couldn't eat. She sipped unhappily at her tankard of ginger beer. At last she said, 'I have a very strong feeling it's going to be dangerous to go on, but I simply can't do anything else. If anyone wants to turn back, I'll understand.'

Rowanne bristled. 'We've been through all this. Can't we just eat in peace for once? Unless you'd *rather* I went?' she added icily. 'Then you can find the Ring and keep it for yourself!'

Fleabag glared over the tabletop from his place on Phelan's knee. 'How *dare* you?' he spat. 'Watch her, Phelan, I don't trust that so-called knight the length of a fishbone.'

He ducked under the table and measured how far he'd have to spring to catch Rowanne's leg with a well-sharpened claw he'd been saving, just in case.

Phelan whispered in Fleabag's ear. 'She's just frightened, like the rest of us. Would you slip round the back and see what the local cats have to say? I feel just as nervous about this place as Gemma does, and I'd quite like to know what we're walking into.'

With silken smoothness, Fleabag slid from Phelan's

lap, but before he could emerge from under the table, the inn door thudded open and a troop of soldiers marched into the room.

The sergeant, a tall, red-haired man in immaculate bright blue uniform and sporting a huge moustache, thumped the bar and roared, 'Well, are there any volunteers this year?'

The travellers looked around in astonishment. But apart from themselves and the soldiers, the room was suddenly quite empty.

30 Prison!

The dungeon was extremely cold. Foetid water drip-dripped from the vaulted ceiling to a heap of rotting hay.

The friends huddled together in a corner that stank of stale urine. Their chains chaffed and rattled every time they moved.

'This is all my fault,' Gemma groaned. 'You all trusted me because of a silly nagging idea in my head.

Rowanne buried her head in her hands. 'If only I'd been armed, I'd have saved us all.'

'Look, it's clear it's me they're after,' Phelan argued. 'Someone's recognized me – they must think you're all part of my criminal gang. I'm sorry.'

'Oh stop moaning, all of you,' Fleabag scolded. 'There're plenty of good rats down here, we could have some fun chasing them if you'd only pipe down and not scare them off.'

Just then, something rattled in the hay.

Sinking low, Fleabag wriggled his tail, pulled back his whiskers and pounced. After a short struggle a grey corpse lay on its back, eyes staring blankly and pink paws curled.

Ten minutes later there were three.

Fleabag strode around them proudly, tail erect and whiskers splayed.

No one commented.

'Aren't you going to tell me how brilliant I am?' he sulked.

'NO!' they shouted in chorus.

So for once, Fleabag shut up.

The night was long, dark and frightening.

At dawn, bolts were drawn and keys screeched in an ancient lock. The door opened slowly and heavy footsteps heralded a thickset, bald man with no teeth. He put a loaf and a jug of water on the floor, right under the drips from the ceiling.

The gaoler straightened and grinned. 'So you're the volunteers. Well done. Most public-spirited of you, I must say! Congratulations! I hope you have a nice time at the festival.'

Struggling against the clanking manacles on his wrists, Phelan clambered to his feet. 'What *is* happening? Volunteers for what? Why are we here? We haven't done anything wrong.'

Rowanne also tried to stand, but her chain was too short. 'I demand you tell us what's happening. I am the Lady-Knight Rowanne de Montiland of the Queen's Guard. You must release me and my companions immediately!'

The man grinned and bowed. 'Pleased to meet you, I'm sure, your ladyship. Now I'm sorry, I must go and see to the other lords and ladies in my care. So much to do, so little time!'

As he was about to close the door the gaoler caught sight of Fleabag's hunting trophies. His face lit up and with one scoop, he tucked the cat under his arm. 'Now you are what I call a useful sort. I'll keep you. He won't get *you*, no, he won't, puss.'

To everyone's amazement, Fleabag did not protest, but purred and snuggled up to his new master. The key turned and they were alone again.

Gemma sniffed and wiped her nose on her sleeve.

Phelan took her hand and said, 'Fleabag would never desert us. He probably thinks he'll help us best if he's free.'

'I'm sure you're right,' Gemma replied. 'But he

went without even a goodbye lick.'

Rowanne was examining her chains. 'If I had my dagger, I'm sure I could force one of these links. They're heavy but not particularly well made.'

'If I had a dagger I could pick the locks,' muttered Phelan. 'In fact, I could probably do it with a hairpin.' He looked hopefully at Rowanne.

She rummaged under her woollen snood and pulled one out. 'Will this do?'

'Perfect!' and he began on Rowanne's wrist manacle. 'I'm starting with you because you're the best fighter,' he explained. 'I'll do Gemma next. If you get a chance to run before I'm free, then go. And may the Ring Fire light your way.'

Gemma did not know what to say. She couldn't imagine running away without Phelan.

For a long time he worked in silence. The only sounds were the scratching of wire against iron and the dripping of water right onto their breakfast bread. 'Almost got it!' he whispered, but before he could snap the lock open, the thump of feet along the stone corridor made him drop the pin.

Seconds later, a sharp command halted a column of soldiers outside. The keys jangled and the door swung reluctantly on its hinges.

The bald gaoler came in and undid the chains.

'Time to go now, boys and girls,' he said cheerfully. 'You didn't eat the breakfast I cooked for you so loving-like. Tut, tut, that's a waste now, isn't it? Still, you won't need it where you're going.'

Next to him the sergeant barked, 'Get up!' and Gemma and Phelan found themselves jerked to their feet.

Rowanne jumped up, about to demand her rights once more, when she caught sight of Fleabag in the open doorway. She signaled to him, but he pretended to ignore her.

As they were marched out, Fleabag slipped between their feet. Leaving the gaoler calling, 'Puss, puss? Nice bit o'fish I bin and bought for you. Here, puss!'

Fleabag skilfully matched his step with the soldiers then leaped into Gemma's arms.

She buried her face in his warm fur. 'Thank goodness you're back. I'm scared,' she whispered.

'So you should be,' he replied. 'I've had a chat with the gaoler's dog and I've found out what's going on.'

The prisoners were bundled into a wagon.

Bars were put up to prevent their escape and a thick oilcloth was thrown over the top so they could see nothing outside. When they were secure, the wagon trundled away, the iron-clad wheels clattering over cobbles. Soon the noise gave way to a softer sound. 'Mud,' said Rowanne. 'We're out in the country again.'

'Good, then it's safe to talk.' Fleabag jumped down and sat in the middle, where they could all hear him. 'Now, there's a beast in these parts – I don't know what it is exactly, but many years ago it used to devour all the sheep and cattle for miles around. The story goes that long ago, a hero lured it into the depths of an ancient cavern, took its powers away and chained it up.

'By evil magic it regained its strength, then a few years ago it broke free and returned to its old ways.'

Fleabag twitched his whiskers. 'The prince of this province pleaded with it to go away, and offered it sheep and cattle, but it demanded humans to eat.

'In the end, the monster agreed to only feed once a year, when it comes out of winter hibernation... At the Spring Festival.'

'How many humans does it eat?' Gemma gasped.

'The dog says it's usually only one adult or two or three children,' Fleabag explained. 'The people of Beulothin agreed to its demands. They think a once-a-year sacrifice is better than having the beast running amok and doing what it pleases. Apparently more

258

people used to die from simply being in the beast's way, than by the annual meal.'

'That's terrible!' Rowanne thumped her fist on the seat. 'Let me at it with a good sword and I will rid the land of this plague!'

'They've tried,' Fleabag replied, 'but it's plated with steely scales so thick with slime, no sword can even scratch them.'

Rowanne was about to interrupt again, but Fleabag held up a paw. 'Before the Spring Festival, lots are drawn to choose that year's victims. Many people have lost loved ones.'

'No wonder everyone's so sad,' said Gemma.

'But any strangers in the land are put at the top of the list. The people aren't inhospitable, but obviously they want to protect their own friends and families.'

Phelan whistled. 'And we walked right into it.'

The friends looked at each other in the gloom. 'I'm so sorry,' Gemma whispered again.

Phelan and Rowanne both took one of her hands and squeezed her fingers.

'You did what you believed was right,' Phelan whispered.

Suddenly the wagon jerked to a halt.

Fleabag darted under Gemma's cloak.

The black oilcloth was hauled back and dazzling

daylight streamed in. Guards in purple uniforms tugged away the iron bars and tail-board.

'Out!' ordered the sergeant. 'Quick about it.'

The friends found themselves outside a low grey stone building with tiny windows. Phelan's heart sank, for to one side carpenters were busily constructing what could only have been a scaffold.

The guards prodded the prisoners with sticks, driving them through a dark doorway and down slippery steps. Their new prison was small and square. Bread, water, a bucket and a pile of blankets had been left out for them.

Gemma handed the blankets around, then wrapping herself in one, she curled up in a corner.

Phelan came and sat next to her. 'We're not dead yet,' he said gently. 'Show us the Ring Fire, Gemma. We all need it.'

She opened her trembling hands.

There was no flame!

'No!' Gemma gasped.

But just then the door opened again.

'Which one of you is the lady de something?' demanded the sergeant's stern, military voice.

Rowanne jumped to her feet. 'I am the Lady Rowanne de Montiland and I demand to see your Prince. It is *outrageous* to imprison us. He will be made to apologise.'

The man looked her up and down. 'I don't know about you seeing *him*, but he'll see *you*. You're first. Tomorrow at dawn.'

Then he turned to the others. 'If the beast goes away after that, the rest of you will be free. If he doesn't, then the next day it's you – then you,' he jerked a thumb at Phelan and Gemma in turn. Then he glared at Fleabag. 'We'll even use the cat if we have to.'

'How could you feed a monster with innocent people?' Phelan demanded. 'It's heartless.'

The sergeant's face was grim. 'How? Easy. If the beast ain't full after munching you lot up, my little boy is next.'

He span smartly on his heel and left, slamming the door behind him.

Gemma lifted her head from her blanket. 'Queen Sophia told me there'd been no dragons in the land for many years. I wonder if it's the same one come back and people only thought it was dead?'

'I bet she became queen because she was the one who got rid of it,' said Phelan. 'It's just the sort of thing she'd have done.'

'That's just what did happen,' Fleabag said, then he buried his nose under his tail and closed his eyes.

They all dozed off, to be woken by Rowanne retching into the bucket.

'Are you all right?' Gemma asked.

Rowanne lifted her head. 'I'm nervous before a battle, but not frightened. I've never really known fear. But this time... I... I think it's because I'll have no weapons tomorrow. When I've got a sword in my hands, it feels like an even match. But the thought of being chained up – just waiting to be eaten, I can't stand it.'

And she collapsed into hysterical sobbing.

The others sat in silence, just watching and listening. There was nothing left to say.

31 A Bad Night

Gemma lay awake all night, staring into the dark.
A few hours before dawn, her teeth began to chatter.

'Are you cold?' Phelan whispered.

'F-frozen,' Gemma stuttered. 'Fleabag's keeping my knees warm, it's my back.'

Phelan pushed his jacket across the floor to her. 'Take it,' he whispered. 'I'm not too bad.'

'Are you sure?'

'Honestly. I'd like you to use it,' he replied.

Gemma pulled the coat on, but sleep still did not come. She was almost warm enough, but there was an uncomfortable lump against her spine, and however she twisted, she could not shift it.

At last Fleabag got up in disgust. 'Even a condemned cat needs beauty sleep!' he moaned, curling up next to Phelan.

Soon the blue-grey of first light crept in through a grating above their heads. Phelan knelt by Rowanne and lifted the blanket from her face.

Then he crept beside Gemma and sat next to her. 'Are you awake?'

'Yes.'

'I'm going to take Rowanne's place. I'm sure the beast won't care whether he gets a knight or a thief. I'm taller than her so there's a chance I might fill him up better.'

Gemma looked at him with wide eyes.

He shrugged. 'Rowanne can't do it. I've never seen anyone as terrified as she is. If I go, it gives you three another full day to think of a way out of this mess.' Phelan held out his hand. 'Goodbye, Gemma. Thanks for helping me to become myself.'

Gemma took his hand.

At last she managed to find her voice. 'But you've always been frightened of beasts – wolves and things. And the scaffold is your worst nightmare because of your parents...'

Phelan smiled gently. 'Dread eats into your heart and mind so you can't function any more. I've realized I'm not afraid of death, but I have been dreading how it'll happen.'

He hugged his knees. 'It's funny, but now the dread has gone away, I can do what I have to do.'

Gemma closed her eyes and hid her face inside Phelan's coat. It smelled comforting.

'And I keep thinking about the other people,' Phelan went on. 'People like that soldier's boy, who'll be next. I might be able to give them another year, and maybe a hero will come. The new king maybe?'

He gave Gemma a hug. 'All I ask is that you'll take any chance to escape. Don't martyr yourself in memory of me or anything stupid. You of all people must get back. Who knows what crook or tyrant may be holding the Ring at this very moment? Promise me you'll be sure the holder is a true king or queen. And Rowanne – she must get back too. She must speak for the people who are suffering across the land. So run the moment you can. Promise?'

Gemma's voice stuck in her throat, so she just nodded.

Phelan hesitated. 'I've got two more favours to ask.'

'Anything.'

'Will you light a little of the Ring Fire for me when I'm out there? It will help me go through with it.'

'If the Fire will burn at all, I will hold it till I drop, like the Fire Wielder.'

'And the last thing...' Phelan looked sheepish.

'Yes?'

'Can I have my coat back? I'm freezing.'

Gemma laughed, although she wanted to cry. She pulled the jacket from her shoulders and passed it over. 'There's a funny lump in the lining. It kept me awake all night.'

Just then the sound of footsteps echoed along the passageway. 'Light the Fire now,' whispered Phelan. 'Let me see it before I go.'

For a few seconds he watched the flickering glow between Gemma's fingers. Then he sighed and stood to attention next to the door, waiting for the moment it would open.

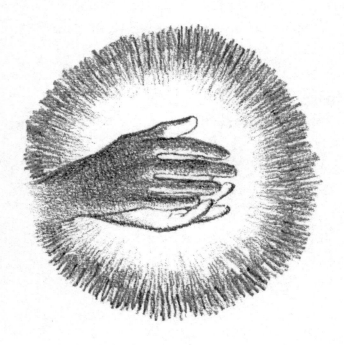

32 The Dragon

At dawn on the Spring Festival every man, woman, child and animal was safely barricaded in cellars and barns. No one moved or spoke lest the beast should come their way. The reek of its breath seeped under doors and around loose window frames.

The sun rose, only to be smothered by a pall of cloud. Out of the gloom a serpent-shape twisted its way across the skies. Blood-red scales glinted in the light of its own fire and two thundering wings beat the air with searing heat.

But the only ones who saw the monster approaching were Phelan, chained by the waist to his scaffold, and from the top window of the prison, a thin, grey man.

Prince Tomas of Beulothin was dressed in funereal black and unashamedly weeping to see yet another man die. In recent years the dragon had demanded more and more victims. Did the dungeon hold enough prisoners to satisfy its appetite?

Tomas knew that one day he must at last take off his crown and step forward himself – or the whole land would be laid to waste.

'But what then?' he whispered, 'who will protect my people once I am gone?'

Phelan couldn't help trembling as he watched the beast come closer. 'Keep the Fire burning, Gemma,' he shouted. 'I need its warmth. Keep it alight, please.'

In the darkness below, Gemma realized she could see pictures in the flames, just as she'd done in the queen's Ring, almost a year ago. And at last she knew who the people were...

Phelan and Rowanne.

The scene shifted and now she saw only Phelan, chained and alone.

She wished she'd given him the tiny flame for comfort. Would it have worked? It was too late now.

The ground shook as the dragon landed. It scraped its rattling scales across the fields, scorching the earth and leaving trails of burning slime.

With thudding feet it approached the scaffold, sweeping its tail from side to side, its five eyes glaring hungrily at Phelan.

It stopped to lick its fangs and consider its prey.

High in the sky, three large birds were circling, screaming and scolding.

'Go away,' Phelan yelled. 'You can't help me, *shoo*!'

The beast crept closer. Steam and smoke belched from his nostrils.

Phelan's eyes watered as he struggled to breathe through the stench.

The dragon stretched its jaws and took another step, just as the birds dived at its head, cawing noisily.

Two flapped at its eyes, while the third flew right between its jaws and dropped something dark and glinting between its teeth.

The dragon roared and snapped, but all three ravens soared away, leaving one black feather drifting in the foul gasses.

Inside the prison, Gemma still watched in the Fire. She held her breath. Had the birds come to save Phelan?

She tried to make the Fire glow more brightly, but it only faded.

'No!' she gasped, not now, *please*.'

Then the pictures of Phelan came into her mind, strong and clear. The Ring Fire was burning *inside* her as Phelan had said it would.

She had become one with it.

Standing in the middle of the dismal prison, Gemma opened her hands. As the Fire grew, she surrounded Phelan with its glow.

In her mind she saw the birds had gone, but Phelan

was standing straight and still. Dread was pulsing all around him.

'Be strong, the Ring Fire is with you,' she whispered. 'Think of it so you know what to do.'

'Thank you,' she heard him say.

Outside, the dragon forgot the birds, and swung its massive head towards it prey once more.

But Phelan didn't notice, he was too busy rummaging in his coat pocket to think about being afraid.

'*Concentrate*!' Gemma urged.

'Got it!' Phelan shouted, pulling out something small and knobbly.

Clenching his fist, he watched the beast's ponderous approach.

Its sulphurous breath seared Phelan's lungs.

The monster sniffed, then flicked its lurid purple tongue. Its bulbous eyes rolled as its tooth-laden jaws yawned and crunched.

Stretching its scraggy neck, the dragon shuffled closer, dribbling drool…

Gemma held the picture of Phelan surrounded by the Ring Fire. She kept it steady. She daren't let it waver for one moment.

Phelan seemed to be measuring the distance. Waiting. Calculating.

The beast opened its maw and belched.

Choking and retching, Phelan swung back his arm and threw a small brown lump right down the cavernous throat.

The creature swallowed… then looked surprised.

It flung back its head to roar, but only a feeble splutter came out.

Swinging its head low, it snaked around Phelan and opened its dribbling jaws again.

But this time…

Scalding black blood spewed out.

The dragon tossed its head from left to right. Its back arched high, then crashed down on the scaffold, splintering it from end to end.

Phelan was left hanging like a puppet in chains.

But still the beast did not attack.

Instead it writhed, slamming its huge body against the prison walls, rolling and crashing. Its agonized bellow echoed from the hills to the mountains beyond.

At last the dragon was panting on its side, lashing its tail weakly. Slowly the steam and stench subsided. The beast twitched, then lay still. It was as long as twenty carriages and as tall as a house. Final wisps of putrid air gasped from its lungs.

It was dead.

A word from prince Tomas, and soldiers swarmed below. Drawing their swords, they hacked at the beast's head but to no avail.

Within moments, the prince was at Phelan's side unlocking the chains that bound his waist.

Dizzily, Phelan sank to the ground, where he sat staring at the body of the beast.

'Deathcap,' he murmured.

'What?' asked the prince.

'Deathcap toadstool. I lost one in the lining of my coat months ago, but I found it this morning. Just as the dragon was about to attack, a raven flew past and dropped something – that's what gave me the idea. I thought that if the beast couldn't be hurt from the *outside*, than perhaps I could kill it from the *inside*.'

The prince shook his head. 'I've heard of deathcap, but I didn't realize it worked *that* quickly.'

Then Phelan grinned. 'Good job, though.' And with that, he sagged to the ground.

Soldiers hurried to the basement and flung the prison door open. Gemma dashed out with Fleabag hot on her heels.

Daylight had never felt so wonderful. The

poisonous blackness thinned and blew away in the morning breeze and the sun came out.

Gemma ran to the beast's head and looked into its blank, yellow eyes.

Phelan staggered to his feet and stood beside her. 'I want to see what that raven dropped.'

'What do you mean?' Gemma asked.

Still wobbly from his ordeal, Phelan stumbled to the other end of the snout and plucked a slimy lump from between the dragon's teeth.

'Yuck!' he wiped the thick saliva on his breeches.

'What is it?' Gemma asked.

'I don't know, some sort of a cube with gold edging.' Phelan pushed his fingernail into a crack. 'It doesn't open, it's solid.'

He handed it to Gemma who turned it over and

shook it, then gave it back. 'What is it?'

Phelan shrugged and slipped it into his pocket. 'Part of a puzzle maybe? But I'd like to keep it as a memento, watching those birds drop it gave me the idea that saved my life.'

Tomas inclined his head. 'Sir, you are welcome to anything in my power to give. But first, my men are bringing gun powder to dispose of this fiend, would you care to stand back?'

'May I do it?' Gemma asked.

The prince spread his hands. 'You? How?'

'Like this.' Gemma stepped forward and placed a flame of the Ring Fire onto the dragon's greasy head.

With a *whoomph*, the whole creature caught light and burned.

33   The Wolf Prince

When Phelan awoke, he was in a gold painted bed in a magnificent chamber in the palace of Beriot.

Next to him sat Gemma and Rowanne, dressed in fresh clothes and tucking into a sumptuous meal.

Fleabag had begged to be excused because he preferred his fish raw and did not think a posh bedroom was quite the place to enjoy his feast.

'Hello Phelan, try and eat something,' Gemma coaxed. 'There's no deathcap in this, I've checked.'

Phelan grinned weakly and tried to sit. 'Ow! Why do I hurt so much?'

'You've got bad burns from the beast's breath, but you'll be all right,' Rowanne replied. 'First of all, I want to thank you for standing in for me. I never realized I was such a coward before – or such a snob. To think I once wanted you hanged!'

Phelan shook his head. 'Each to his own. I'd be useless in battle. I simply found my dread had gone, and I could meet the monster. I'd forgotten about the deathcap until the last minute.'

'Gemma kept the Ring Fire burning all the time,'

Rowanne told him. 'She *willed* you through it.'

'I could feel it. I think the real thanks goes to Gemma.'

She smiled. 'No, to the Ring Fire and the Fire Giver – and the birds that showed you what to do. Now eat up, someone wants to see you.'

Phelan ate a little, then a servant came and dressed him in a loose silk robe that would not chafe his burns. Painfully he eased himself into a chair and the door opened.

In walked Prince Tomas, attended by sixteen of his advisers. As they entered, they all knelt.

Tomas took off his crown and held it out to Phelan. 'Twenty years ago, when the beast returned, I begged it to go. It told me it would leave forever if I went with it willingly. I thought it was a trick to get me to leave my land unprotected. I never told anyone, but I convinced myself I was needed to rule the province. I was too frightened to dare to look death in the face for the sake of my people.

'I am no longer fit to rule. In the name of our departed queen, and whoever her successor may be, I name you Prince Phelan of Beulothin.'

Phelan stared at Tomas and then at the golden crown that lay cold and heavy in his hands. He turned it over and stared at it blankly. 'I – I don't know what to say. Is this your will also?' he asked the advisers.

An elegant woman robed in emerald satin strode forward and bowed. 'Our prince has served us well and faithfully for many years, but if he wishes to abdicate in favour of one who is braver and will serve his people better than himself, we can only agree. You saved our people. We vow to serve you as loyally and faithfully as our meager skills permit.'

Fleabag had crept in during this discussion and was now licking his whiskers contentedly. 'Now there's an offer you can't refuse,' he mewed. 'The food here is first-rate. I'll stay and be your chief adviser if you like.'

Phelan laughed. 'Two wonderful offers, but I can't accept either because we must leave very soon. My friends and I must return to Harflorum for the presentation of the queen's successor.'

Gemma nodded in agreement.

Tomas looked crestfallen and his advisors murmured disappointedly.

'However,' Phelan went on, 'I am deeply honoured by your invitation. But just because I had an old toadstool in my pocket, doesn't necessarily mean I'll make a good prince. Tomas, you understand your people. You know their needs. Please – keep your crown.'

278

He tried to hand the circlet back.

Tomas was not to be deterred. 'But I have *not* served my people faithfully. I am no prince at all.'

Phelan thought for a moment. 'Very well, if I accept, may I go away to complete my other tasks first?'

The advisers conferred for a few moments. 'Of course, sire,' they agreed heartily.

'Then I will be your prince.'

The advisors cheered.

Phelan held up his hand for silence. 'But I insist on appointing a good regent to stand in my place. Is that acceptable, my lords and ladies?'

'Aye.'

'Certainly sire,' they agreed.

Phelan smiled. 'Then, Tomas of Beulothin, I appoint you as my regent.' He leaned forward and placed the crown firmly back on the prince's grey hair.

As he did so he whispered, 'You'll be a much better prince from now on.'

'Indeed, my lord.'

'Then get up. You have work to do.'

As Tomas stood, his face was wreathed in smiles and the company applauded warmly. 'Tonight we will have a banquet to celebrate Prince Phelan's victory over the dragon. The people have many gifts to give to you, much better ones than pickings from the dragon's teeth. My lords, my ladies, please rest until then.'

'And Cat!' purred Fleabag from his proud seat on Phelan's lap.

'Indeed, your Purrship.' Tomas bowed to Fleabag and left the room with his counsellors in tow.

Gemma and Rowanne exchanged glances, and whistled.

Fleabag spread his whiskers and purred. 'Well, I never, Prince Phelan – the Wolf Prince.'

'I'll present Rowanne with that catfur collar she's always wanted if you ever call me that again,' Phelan laughed, pretending to cuff Fleabag around the ear.

Then he took Gemma's hand. 'You look miserable. Don't worry, I'll come back with you and then after that – who knows? You'll always have a home here, and I swear you'll never have to peel another potato as long as you live.'

'I'm not unhappy,' Gemma replied, rubbing her hands together as if they hurt. 'It's just that I have this awful feeling that I have to go soon, tonight if possible. I don't expect you to come, I'm sure your burns are hurting, but I have to go. The Ring Fire is calling me. It's urgent. We may not have found the Ring, but I am needed.'

Phelan looked from Fleabag to Rowanne, then back to Gemma again. 'You're right. I feel it too.'

Fleabag jumped down from Phelan's lap. 'Shame,' he said. 'The dustbins here are superb.'

34 Return to Harflorum

The hours before the banquet were very busy with preparations for the journey. Prince Tomas gave Rowanne and Phelan good horses and Gemma a sure-footed pony. Fleabag was given a special pannier where he could sleep like a king on a soft fleece.

Supplies were packed but as time was of the essence, only four armed soldiers were readied to protect and guide the party.

It was almost dark when everything was done.

'Can we ride as soon as we've eaten?' Gemma begged.

Rowanne looked out at the night sky. 'No, it's overcast, no moon or stars. We won't be able to see where we're going. We'll ride much faster by day, and it'll be better for the horses too. We'll get some sleep and leave at first light, I promise.'

After a great deal of cajoling and bribing from Gemma, Fleabag permitted his fur to be washed, dried, and combed. He even allowed a scarlet silk ribbon to be tied around his neck.

Rowanne dressed in formal knightly dress: white

silk stockings and knee length breeches, a loose lawn shirt and a cloth-of-gold tabard. Her short cloak was of scarlet satin edged with gold.

Gemma's hair had been cut properly. It had never looked right since 'Auntie' had hacked it in the thieves' kitchen. Now it was neat and shiny. Phelan had given orders that she should wear a long dress of flame-red silk.

'I don't think that's really my colour,' Gemma protested when she was shown the gown, but the soft fabric felt so delicious, she put it on.

Phelan himself would only wear a plain linen shirt

and trousers with a blue woollen waistcoat. His black hair and beard were cut short, curling tightly around his dark face. To please Prince Tomas, he wore the golden circlet of the princedom.

As they met by the dining room door, the four travellers stared at each other in amazement.

'Gemma?' Phelan gasped. 'You look so lady-like!'

She blushed, then whispered, 'and you're all grown up and respectable!'

Phelan laughed out loud.

As they entered the room, trumpets blasted with a long and fancy fanfare. At the sight of their new prince, the guests rose to their feet and the room fell silent.

Lead by Fleabag, his tail high and his whiskers spread proudly, Phelan walked with Rowanne and Gemma through the bowing and curtseying guests to the high table. They sat and the room filled with cheers and applause.

Fleabag was given a fat satin cushion at the end of the high table, where he held court with all the admiring palace cats.

After the food and the speeches, Phelan removed his crown on the pretext that it kept slipping to one side.

There was dancing and merriment. The whole city

was alive with music and fireworks. Flashing bonfires and squealing rockets lit up the night sky from the sea to the mountains.

By midnight, Gemma couldn't stop yawning. 'I must get some sleep,' she whispered to Phelan, do you mind if I leave?'

'No, I'm all-in myself,' he replied. 'We must be on the road in a few hours.'

As Phelan stood to go, Prince Tomas caught him by the arm. 'Before you retire, my lord, we must give you our gifts,' he insisted. 'The people have brought you tokens of gratitude.'

Phelan pulled away in horror. 'But you've made me a prince, given us beautiful clothes and equipped us for our return. That's more than enough.'

'That's nothing!' laughed the Prince leading Phelan into another chamber that was piled high with boxes and packages of every conceivable shape and size.

Phelan blanched. 'I can't possibly... I mean, what would I *do* with it all?'

'Please,' begged the Prince, 'take *something* as a token of our love and gratitude, otherwise the people will be offended.'

Phelan sighed. 'My friends may choose what they will, but I beg you, take everything here, sell it and use the money to help the poor – and I want a large purse of gold to go once a year to a man called Aelforth in Rupertsberg, I will send directions of where he lives.'

'As you wish, my lord,' Tomas replied. He looked a little surprised, but nodded to a servant who made a note of the name.

Phelan rubbed his eyes. 'There is more here than any man could even *look* at in one lifetime – let alone *possess*. Let me sleep now and I give my word I will take something back from Beulothin.'

As the first light softened the black curves of the countryside, Gemma was up and dressed in new travelling clothes. They were very much like her old ones but warmer and with no holes. The Queen's shoes were too tight and they leaked, so she packed them with her other gear as she could not bear to part with them.

Rowanne appeared at her door. She too had fresh riding clothes but best of all, a bright, new sword hung at her side with a matching dagger. 'Personal gifts from Phelan,' she grinned. 'I think we're even now.'

Outside in the courtyard they were met by Fleabag, who had made a special effort to get his fur comfortably matted again.

'You're a mess,' Rowanne chided. 'You almost looked respectable last night.'

Fleabag rolled over and wriggled, adding another knot or two. 'It's so you'll never have my hide round your neck. I've acquired some particularly itchy fleas here. Would you like one?'

Ignoring him, Rowanne mounted her horse, and the company rode through the palace gates.

Even at that early hour, a cheering crowd was gathered. Prince Tomas and his guards escorted them to the city walls. There were no lengthy farewells; Gemma's sense of urgency would not permit it.

Rowanne was a little grumpy. She had enjoyed the fuss that had been made of her and longed to spend time in the Prince's stables or jousting with some of the knights in the practice yard.

At first they made good progress. The soldiers accompanying them set up tents at night, so no time was lost looking for accommodation. When the spring rains came they were forced to stop in a small village as floods swept across the low-lying ground and cut them off for a whole week.

At last they took to the road again. Sunshine dried the lanes and warmed the blossomy hedgerows. The air smelled richly of summer as they reached

Rupertsberg. The party skirted the walls, then gathering speed, they galloped up the next hill and through the wood where Phelan's gang had first attacked.

The ex-thief looked neither to his right nor to his left. He bowed his head over his horse's mane and rode on.

One afternoon, they came over a ridge and saw Harflorum ahead. The city crowned a low hill, overlooking wide plains that rolled to the south. The scent of hawthorn filled the air and gardens were abundant with early roses. Everything looked peaceful.

Inside the walls, Harflorum's streets were crammed with noisy, shoving crowds from every corner of the kingdom.

The streets stank of bodies as people jostled and pushed. Thieves plied their trade, as did peddlers with trays of imitation opal rings and fire jugglers breathing 'real Ring Fire' from their noses and mouths. Mothers struggled to get frightened children through the crush.

Everywhere was turmoil.

The friends eased their horses through the throng until they reached the palace. Rowanne leaned over and gave her name to a guard who did not know her.

'I don't care who you are; you take your place with the rest. The queue goes right round the palace. Just have to be patient.' Then he turned her horse's head and slapped the animal on the flank.

The frightened mare reared and tried to bolt, but Rowanne controlled it with a tight rein. 'This is hopeless,' she yelled above the hubbub. She beckoned the soldiers who had accompanied them. 'Take the mounts and find somewhere to sleep outside the city. This is no place for anyone who doesn't need to be here. We'll send for you in a few days.' The men saluted and led the horses back through the mêlée.

Gemma kept close behind Rowanne. The crush frightened her. Crowds made her feel as if she couldn't breathe. *No fainting this time*, she told herself firmly.

Phelan carried Fleabag on his shoulder, and he found himself eye-ball to eye-ball with Rowanne. 'What do we do now, clever-clogs?' the cat yowled.

Rowanne scowled at him. 'Make yourself useful – jump down and find a way into the palace.'

'Good idea – for once,' he replied, leaping to the ground. Within moments, he had dodged the nearest feet and disappeared.

'What's everyone queuing for, anyway?' Phelan

yelled at Rowanne.

A short fat woman with a water bottle and a cup overheard. 'Don't you know what's goin' on? Goodness me and love-a-duck!' she tutted. 'Where you fine folks bin this past year? These 'ere people are wantin' to show their opal rings to the Fire Wielder.'

She snorted with laughter. 'They all thinks they's got the true Ring.' She nudged Rowanne in the ribs and chortled. 'Trouble is, he's very weak. He's dyin', and he's certainly too far gone to see folks, so we's all just sittin' 'ere. Only got to wait until tomorrer though, then the year and a day's up! But on the bright side, I's doin' all right.'

She turned to Gemma. 'Want a drink, dearie?'

'No, thank-you,' she replied. 'What happens at the end of tomorrow if he still can't see anyone?'

The woman shrugged and her three chins wobbled. 'Dunno. There'll be a big fight, I s'ppose. I won't stick around, that's for sure.' She turned to the next person behind them. 'Buy a drink, dearie?'

Just then Fleabag came panting back and jumped back into Phelan's arms. 'I've found a way to get into the palace through the kitchen. Someone's left the garden gate open. But the bad news is that Cook is there – in a filthy temper.'

Gemma winced, but Rowanne, who'd heard all

about Cook's ways, pulled herself up to her full height. 'Come on, Cat!' she said, 'Let's have Cook for supper, shall we?'

They wriggled and squeezed their way through the crowds until they reached the wall around the vegetable garden. As Fleabag had said, the gate was slightly ajar. They ran across the neat beds of beans and herbs and Phelan pushed open the kitchen door.

Cook, who had been beating one of the kitchen boys, stopped and looked up at the intruders. He dropped the unfortunate lad on the floor and brandished his rolling pin. 'Get out! This is private!'

With a chilling yowl, Fleabag sprang with claws

splayed. He caught Cook right on the face. At the same moment, Phelan wrested the rolling pin from his fist.

Cook thrashed and bellowed.

Gemma picked Fleabag off while Rowanne twisted Cook's arm behind his back. Ignoring his yelling and kicking, she marched him out of the kitchen, along the garden path and shoved him through the garden door and into the gutter.

Phelan slammed and locked the door with a satisfied sigh. 'He's not getting back in *here*!' he grinned.

When Phelan and Rowanne turned around, they saw they were surrounded by kitchen staff staring with open mouths. As they stepped back into the kitchen, applause broke out.

Fleabag excused himself and went to have a quick look at his favourite dead rat, to see whether it was ready to eat after having matured behind Cook's chair for a whole year.

Gemma led the way up the back stairs where she and Fleabag used to talk.

On the first floor, they ran straight into the butler. 'What the hell do you think…' he began.

But Rowanne shoved him aside. 'This way,' she said, turning left and leaping up the next flight of stairs to the top of the palace.

At the end of the next corridor was the Hall of Light.

With a pounding heart and a dry mouth, Gemma asked, 'What are we going to say? We've nothing to show him.'

35 The King and the Fire Wielder

Let's at least tell him we tried,' said the cat putting a paw on the door.

Gemma turned the handle.

'You can't go in there,' yelled a stern voice from behind them.

Rowanne swung round. It was the captain of the Queen's Guard. She stood to attention and saluted smartly. 'Sir!' she said, 'I have escorted this company on an errand at the Fire Wielder's request. He will want to see us.'

The captain relaxed as he recognized Rowanne. 'I'm sorry,' he said quietly. 'It's impossible. The Fire Wielder is dying. It won't be much longer.'

'But he expressly ordered me...' Rowanne protested.

The captain crossed his arms and stood his ground. 'Lady-knight de Montiland, I said, *no*.'

Rowanne drew her sword and said, 'Sir, I have never disobeyed you, but this time, I must.'

The captain drew his sword too, and the two took their positions for a duel.

Seeing his chance, Fleabag patted Gemma's leg. 'Psst… Rowanne's enjoying herself – she'll be fine.' Then he pressed both front paws on the heavy carved door and pushed.

Gemma and Fleabag stepped into the Hall of Light.

Phelan stood uncertainly on the threshold, but Gemma beckoned him to follow. The room was silent, filled with the soft glow of the early summer evening.

Asleep on a settee, just as they had left him a year ago, lay the Fire Wielder. He had become very thin, his cheeks sunken and his conker-brown skin had turned sallow.

On the table next to him, in a little silver dish, burned a weak flame, not much bigger than a glowing match head. All that was left of the Ring Fire.

'Oh dear,' said Gemma, 'I must have used it all up.'

'Quick,' Phelan urged. 'I hear more guards coming.'

At this, Fleabag jumped onto the Fire Wielder's chest and licked his face. 'Wake up, sir,' he said. 'We're back!'

The old man moaned, opened his eyes and smiled. 'I dreamt you were coming,' he whispered. 'I hoped it was true.' He held out a shaking hand. 'Give me the

Ring – we'll put the Fire back straight away.'

'We haven't got it, sir,' Gemma hung her head. 'Everything went wrong. I've failed.'

'Nonsense!' snapped the old man, lifting his head from the pillow. He waved a finger at Phelan. 'You there, you've got it.'

Bemused, Phelan emptied his pockets of a penknife, some string, a candle end and wrapped in a dirty handkerchief was the slimy wooden cube.

'Where did you get that?' the Fire Wielder demanded.

Phelan explained.

'So, you took it from the jaws of death while defending your friends and the people of Beulothin?'

Phelan reddened. 'It wasn't quite that grand sir…'

'Where only a king or queen would dare to look?' The Fire Wielder chuckled. 'Open it!'

'But I can't sir, it's only a…' Phelan began, then he noticed the crack in the side had widened. Carefully he eased the split further apart. Inside, on a bed of sea-green velvet, lay the queen's Ring.

Gemma and Phelan gasped and exchanged glances.

'Give it here, boy,' said the Fire Wielder, opening his hand. 'And Gemma, pass me the Ring Fire… Gently, it's very faded.'

She picked up the tiny flicker of flame. For one

awful second she thought it had gone out, but it steadied at her touch.

The Fire Wielder tried to hold the Ring in one hand, and the Fire in the other, but his fingers fell uselessly onto the quilt that covered him.

'You'll have to do it for me, child,' he said. 'Just let the Flame flow into the stone.'

Gemma took the Ring and let the Fire roll like a glistening bead into the milky-blue opal.

As the two touched, the Ring sprang into a thousand shades of greeny-blue with an orange-red fame at their heart.

'There, that's right! Now,' the Fire Wielder's voice was barely audible, 'put the Ring on the boy's finger. What's your name, lad?'

'Phelan, Sir.'

'Phelan, do you swear to be a good king and to

serve your people faithfully all your days?'

Aghast, Phelan opened his mouth but could not speak.

'Go on! Do you?' Fleabag prompted.

Phelan gulped. 'Yes, sir, I do.'

'Well, that's settled.' The old man let his head loll back on his pillow, but his bright eyes held Gemma in their gaze. 'And you, Gemma by name, Gem by nature, do you swear to carry the Ring Fire so that Phelan here will always have true light to see by, as he rules the land?'

Gemma swallowed hard. *'Me?'*

'You've carried the Ring Fire all year. No one else has had any practice. It's *got* to be you! Gemma Fire Wielder, the latest of our line. Carry it well.'

Phelan nudged her.

Her heart pounded and her mouth went dry. 'Yes,' she replied quietly. 'I swear.'

'Well, that's all right then,' he sighed, closing his eyes and smiling. 'Everything done. Now I can sleep.'

Gemma held the old man's hand. His breathing scarcely flickered in his chest.

'He won't wake again, I'm afraid,' Phelan said softly.

'But what happens now?' Gemma asked.

'I think maybe you ought to speak to your visitors?'

298

Fleabag interrupted. 'Er… there does seem to be rather a lot of them.'

Gemma and Phelan turned to see the room was full of court officials led by the prime minister and the captain of the Guard. Standing in front of them all, beaming with delight, stood the lady-knight Rowanne de Montiland.

She pulled her sword from its sheath and knelt before Phelan, offering the hilt to the young king. 'My lord,' she said. 'My life and my sword are yours.'

There was a murmur of steel and a rustle of clothes as one by one, everyone in the room followed suit.

Gemma started to kneel as well, but Fleabag stopped her. 'Don't, you silly girl. *You're* the Fire Wielder. You hold the flame high for everyone to see.'

Gemma lifted one arm and in her hand, the Fire burned until it filled the evening-darkened room with glorious golden-red light.

When she looked around, even Phelan was on his knees.

'All homage to the Ring Fire,' the king declared, 'in which we live and move and have our being.'

36 Coronation

The next few hours were a blur to Gemma. Everyone wanted to make a fuss of her – especially the butler who had kicked her so viciously when she had been a mere kitchen-maid.

She and Phelan were taken away by lords and ladies-in-waiting, bathed and dressed in the finest robes, but Fleabag made himself scarce when a maid threatened him with a flea comb.

'I suffered all that in Beulothin,' he wailed. 'I swear it cost at least one of my nine lives.'

Gemma looked ruefully out of the palace windows and watched children playing in the gardens. At that moment she would have given anything to be with them, running free and scruffy across the grass.

When she saw her heavy red and gold embroidered dress laid out on the bed, she winced and bit her lip. She remembered how hot and uncomfortable the old Fire Wielder had been the first time they had met.

She turned to the maid who was dressing her.

'I'm not going to wear these,' she announced. 'I've

been carrying the Ring Fire for a year and a day, and I never needed heavy robes to do it – so I'm not going to start now.' With that she pulled on her old trousers and shirt, ran from the room and disappeared down the servants' stairs into the garden.

As she ran past a tangled rambling rose, a dark figure reached out and grabbed her. 'Psst, under here!'

Gemma wriggled beside Phelan. He looked as miserable as she felt. He was wearing a formal suit of padded satin and an itchy-looking lace shirt. 'This means the end of all our fun – all our freedom,' he sighed. 'They've been lecturing me on how a king is expected to behave – all these *rules*. I won't be able to stand it. I wish I'd known before I made my vow to the Fire Wielder. I'd have said "no".'

They squatted side by side under the bush and looked at the gardens with their high walls and railings.

'It's like being in a posh prison,' Gemma tugged at her hair miserably. Then she jumped as thorns pricked into her back.

But it wasn't the rose. It was Fleabag.

'Who do you think made the rules in the first place?' the cat enquired. 'Who thought of all those silly clothes and stuffy rules?'

'Other kings and other Fire Wielders, I suppose.'

'So who would have the authority to *unmake* the rules?' Fleabag persisted.

Phelan sprang up and looked at Gemma with glee. 'Why, *us*, of course!' He took her hands and pulled her onto the grass, swinging her around until they tripped and fell into a dizzy, laughing tumble, rolling all the way down the sloping lawn.

When at last they stopped, all muddied and grass-stained, they were met by a circle of wide-eyed children, staring down at the new King and Fire Wielder in amazement.

Within seconds a valet and two ladies' maids came swooping down from the palace armed with sponges, towels and royal robes, all clicking their tongues.

'Oh, go away!' Phelan laughed. 'From now on, when we're not doing something that we really have to dress up for, we're just going to be ourselves!'

That evening, the old Fire Wielder died.

Gemma did wear an extremely heavy gold and red embroidered robe for his funeral. Solemnly she led the procession from the palace to the graveyard on the sunny slope behind the city. Although she was sad at having lost someone so special, she knew he was glad to be sleeping in the Quiet Place. He had been so tired.

After the funeral was over she took her robes off

and sent her servants away. Fleabag joined her in a window seat, where they sat together. 'You dear, ugly old thing,' she sniffed, stroking his fur.

'More of the dear and less of the ugly and old,' he mewed.

Then they curled up together and cried until a flame-red sunset burned the evening sky with livid fire.

It was there that Phelan found them. He too had taken off his royal robes and told his attendants in no uncertain terms that he wished to be left alone.

The three of them sat quietly hugging each other until the crimson and gold sky faded to indigo.

At last Phelan stood up.

'It's time for bed,' he said gently. 'Tomorrow we have other things to think about.'

The coronation was not held in the throne room – or anywhere in the palace. Phelan insisted that if he were to be king, he must be crowned amongst the people.

On the last day of June, when the sun shone most strongly, an ordinary wooden chair decked with scarlet and yellow ribbon was carried to a large field outside the city. Phelan walked so he could hold the hands of the city children.

Behind him, Gemma rode a cream-coloured pony.

On her lap was a white silk cushion, bearing the royal crown and a plain opal ring with a strong red flame burning at its heart.

She smiled as she waved at the cheering crowd. Everyone wore flowers in their hair and dressed in their best. Music sounded at every corner as buskers and court musicians joined together playing dance music. Soon the city was quite empty, for everyone had flocked to watch the coronation.

As Gemma pushed the Ring onto Phelan's finger, it almost slid off. Phelan and Gemma exchanged worried glances.

Gemma swallowed hard. Who else could possibly be king? The glint of Fire in the opal gave her courage. 'Do you, Phelan, swear to guard and protect your people with all your heart, mind and body?' she asked.

Loudly and clearly, Phelan replied, 'With the help of the Ring Fire, I swear.'

With that, the great Ring tightened gently, clasping his finger, with a friend's reassurance.

Phelan held his hand high, and Fire flashed from the Ring.

The crowds cheered. 'Long live the King!'

'Long live the King,' Gemma replied, lowering the crown onto Phelan's head.

Then the music and dancing and feasting began.

Fleabag, who had permitted Gemma to comb him a little, sat by Phelan's feet and stared up at him.

'Well, you verminous hearthrug, what do you think you're doing?' asked Phelan.

'A cat may look at a king, mayn't he?'

'If he really is a cat, but I've been looking for a fur collar for my friend Rowanne de Montiland and I think you might just do,' teased Phelan, handing his crown to his equerry.

'Oh *her*, sneered the cat, jumping up into the king's lap. 'I hear she's off and away soon?'

Rowanne, who was just bringing Phelan a glass of wine and a large piece of coronation cake, almost tripped on the hem of her long dress.

'What lies are you spreading about me, Cat?' she laughed.

'Only that I hear you're leaving us.'

'I have decided, and my lord king has given his permission, to challenge my disgusting cousin Rupert to face me in fair fight for his princedom.'

Fleabag scratched himself vigorously behind one ear and looked thoughtful. 'I'm coming with you.'

'What?' Gemma couldn't believe her ears. 'I thought you were going to be supervising the installation of central heating in the palace so you'd have warm radiators to sleep on all winter.'

'Plenty of time for that later. Summer's still young.'

'So why do you want to go with Rowanne to Rupertsberg?' Phelan asked.

'Well, if she's going to be challenging that poor, defenceless little man to a contest, I think I'd better go and ensure fair play, don't you?'

'Come off it!' laughed Rowanne. 'You can't expect

me to believe that! And since when did you know anything about fair play? You cheat at every turn!'

Fleabag squinted at the king's Ring as it glowed with the glorious sheen of restored Fire.

'Oh well, I suppose telling a lie ill befits a day like today.' He blushed, as much as a black cat can. 'The truth is, I received word from Rupertsberg this morning that the nice little tortoiseshell in the palace kitchens has consented to be my bride.'

Gemma hugged Fleabag. 'That's wonderful! And I know just the wedding present for you!'

'What?' he asked.

'A can of flea powder!'

Frequently asked Questions:

I often get lovely emails from my readers – here are some of the interesting questions they ask that you might like to know the answer to.

How did you think of 'Fleabag'?

Fleabag is (or was) a real cat – sadly, I doubt if he's still alive.

His name was 'Kapone' and he belonged to friends of mine. I went to see these people one day and their very shaggy black, three-legged cat came up to be stroked. I really like cats, but my friends said, 'Don't let him onto your lap, he's a real fleabag. We've tried everything, combs, powder, drops, but we can't get rid of the fleas.'

At the time, I was trying to think of a story to write, I'd got a few ideas, but nothing was working.

When I met 'Fleabag' I knew I had a hero in the making. The best part was Kapone's owner was a bit of a character – wise, funny, dry, didn't suffer fools gladly... in short, my sort of person.

I put the owner's character into the cat (the person in question does know!) and the story just rolled along nicely after that.

I had huge fun imagining what Fleabag might say and how he'd act.

How did Fleabag lose his leg?

I'm told the real Fleabag (Kapone) lost his leg under a milk lorry at about 6.30 one morning, but if you mean my hero Fleabag – you'll have to read book 3 to find out.

How did you think of the other characters?

Gemma and Phelan were the most unlikely people I could think of to go on a quest. Gemma is a kid from the streets who works hard and is loyal, honest and kind. But she is nobody who becomes Somebody.

I like the idea that everyone is important, we just have to find what it is we are good at and believe in ourselves enough to do it.

Phelan is similar. I didn't plan him; he just appeared in the story and became attached to the quest. It was his idea, and I like him – again, he isn't the sort of hero one might look for – someone who's had a bad start in life and been in trouble.

But people like Phelan are in a good position to be a bit more understanding and kind. I hope so, anyway. Like Gemma, once he overcomes his fears and has the courage to be himself, he blossoms. What about Rowanne? Many stories have a 'knight in shining armour' who helps the quest along. I was feeling mischievous one day and thought I'd have a *lady* knight in shining armour. Then as I wrote her, I discovered she wasn't the sort of assistant most heroes would like to have tagging along.

So poor old Rowanne became a cat-hating snob who's a good soul at heart, but really can't work out her place in things at all, so makes mistakes and has a real tendency to mess things up – especially in book 3!

Do you have any writing tips?

Yes, but there isn't room to put them all down here. You can look up my 'advice to writers' on: www.bethwebb.co.uk/advice-for-writersor, you can come on one of my young people's writing courses: http://www.kilvecourt.co.uk/enrichment/

Happy Writing!

From **Beth** and **Fleabag**